MULK RAJ ANAND

Greatest Short Stories

JAICO PUBLISHING HOUSE

Ahmedabad Bangalore Bhopal Bhubaneswar Chennai
Delhi Hyderabad Kolkata Lucknow Mumbai

Published by Jaico Publishing House
A-2 Jash Chambers, 7-A Sir Phirozshah Mehta Road
Fort, Mumbai - 400 001
jaicopub@jaicobooks.com
www.jaicobooks.com

GREATEST SHORT STORIES
ISBN 81-7224-749-4

First Jaico Impression: 1999
Eleventh Jaico Impression: 2014

Printed by

Contents

Part III: The Social Scene

Part IV: The Comic Vein

Part V: Probing the Mind

Introduction

M.K. NAIK

As the fables in the *Upanishads,* the beast stories in the *Panchatantra* and the Buddhist Jataka tales show, the short story is an art form Indian in origin and yet the paradox is that the modern Indian short story in English is a product of Western influences. From 1898, when 'the first collection of short stories in English by an Indian writer — *Stories from Indian Christian Life* by Kamala Sathianadan — was published'[1] to the present day, the short story has been tackled by most of the leading Indian writers of fiction in English. Among these Mulk Raj Anand is one of the most outstanding, by virtue of his fecundity and the great variety of theme and mood, tone and technique which characterises his short stories.

Mulk Raj Anand has so far produced more than half a dozen collections, of short stories over the last forty years: *The Lost Child and Other Stories* (1934); *The Barber's Trade Union and Other Stories* (1944); *The Tractor and the Corn Goddess and Other Stories* (1947); *Reflections on the Golden Bed and Other Stories* (1953); *The Power of Darkness and Other Stories* (1959); *Lajwanti*

1 C.V. Venugopal, *The Indian Short Story in English: A Survey* (Bareilly, 1975), p.l.

and Other Stories (1966); and *Between Tears and Laughter* (1973). He has, in addition to these, also retold traditional Indian tales in two collections: *Indian Fairy Tales* (1946) and *More Indian Fairy Tales* (1961). This retelling has been, in a sense, a 'tribute of the current to the source', for Anand has, in more than one place, acknowledged his debt to the traditional Indian tales. In his preface to *Indian Fairy Tales,* he observes:

Only by going back to the form of these stories, told by mother to son and son to son, could we evolve a new pattern for the contemporary short story. Of course, the Modern short story is a highly developed folk tale, if it is a folk tale at all. But a revival of the short story form, like the present, seemed to be a fit occasion to relate it to its more primitive antecedents which, surprisingly enough, seem to lie in the source of the sheaf of tales which I have gleaned... Although I have taken in much new psychology into my own writing of the short story, I have always tried to approximate to the technique of the folk tale and the influence of these fairy stories has always been very deep on my short fiction.[2]

The preface to Selected Stories contains an even fuller statement. Characterizing the ancient Indian *Ocean of Stories* as "a symbol of the highly finished art of story-telling in India", Anand adds:

I read it at an early age and was inspired by it to read and hear many of the folk tales told in my country... I wanted to write stories as finished in form and as rich in content as the stories told among my people. In fact, the folk tale form has seemed to me the most perfect form of short story... The folk tales of India... interpret the joys and sorrows of a peasant

2 M.R. Anand, *Indian Fairy Tales* (Bombay, 1946) n.p.

people of the long eras of Indian feudal life. And in spite of the wit, wisdom and morality which they represent, they are not typical of modern sensibility. Therefore, while accepting the form of the folk tale, specially in its fabulous character, I took in the individual and group psychology of the European conte and tried to synthesise the two styles. And thus I sought to create a new kind of fable which extends the old Indian story form into a new age, without the moral lessons of the Indian story, but embodying its verve and vitality and including the psychological understanding of the contemporary period.[3]

Another possible and obviously allied influence was that of his mother. Anand once described his mother an 'illiterate but highly skilled story-teller who could feel a situation passionately.' He recalled an incident. Once, as a boy he was accompanying her, when they met a woman who had just lost her son. Mother stopped to talk to her, but young Anand, getting impatient, hurried her along. When they reached home, she said to him: 'Why did you rush me like that? Didn't you see the dead son of that woman in her eyes?'[4]

Anand has also indicated other possible influences on his short stories:

One of my favourite folk tales was the *Adventures of Raja Rasalu* and I would pester my mother to tell me this over and over again. The humorous anecdotes concocted by one of our teachers, Master Shah Nawaz, based on the legendary incidents in the life of Raja Birbal and Akbar the Great, impressed me with the gift of laughter that one could bring to bear on

---

3 M.R. Anand, *Preface to Selected Stories* (Moscow, 1955), p.5.
4 M.K. Naik, *Mulk Raj Anand* (New Delhi 1973), p.132.

human foibles. When I read some of the stories of Tolstoy in his *Sevestopol Sketches* as well as Gorky's stories, *Creatures That Once Were Men,* I began to conceive the short story as I would write it, by combining the framework of the folk tales with concentration on character and situations of contemporary life. Then I read the fables of Theodore Powys in London and tried to apply the Indian fables of... the *Panchatantra* to my human beings... I adapted the prose poems of Turgenev and my own allegories to the lyric story... Altogether the allegory, the fable, the lyric short story, the satire and the long short story, in my hand, are all, in a peculiar style of my own evolved under various influences, typical of the neo-folk tale, which is my ideal of the short story. The whole concept was built on the hunch that the old Indian short story remains the deepest reference back to various layers of consciousness. Only it had to take in the disintegration of mind and body of the present age and bring flashes of illumination into the dark to reveal layers and under layers of suppressed feelings. The bardic narrative with its moral lesson at the end had to yield to the revelation in which the neo-psychology, which has taken the place of morality, is implicit... What I left for the novel was the epic theme; the story expressed the lyric awareness and a compassionate sense of humour.[5]

In addition to these, Anand's short stories reveal other modes also, such as strong social satire, uproarious laughter and acute psychological perception. The present selection is an attempt to represent the wide range and variety of Anand's short stories. The first group represents the stories of 'Lyric Awareness'. In these stories the element of incident is almost

---

5 Ibid., pp. 132-133.

minimal, the emphasis being an imaginative and emotional apprehension of an aspect of life — either on the human level or on that of animal creation. As in all lyric poetry, the themes here are elemental, such as birth and death, beauty, love and childhood, and the treatment often reveals a symbolic dimension added to realistic presentation. There is also an appropriate heightening of style, in keeping with the mood and the tone of the narrative.

The first story in this *group — The Lost Child* — illustrates almost all these features and is easily one of the most memorable of Anand's short stories. It is a fable in which the traumatic experience of a child also symbolizes the eternal verities of the human condition. The child which has gone to the fair along with its parents wants a toy and a sweet meat and many more things and keeps up a chorus of 'I want'. Then it gets lost, and though friendly hands now offer to it the very things it coveted only a few hours ago, it rejects all of them, all the while crying, 'I want my mother, I want my father, I want my father'. The narrative here moves effortlessly on two levels of significance, even like a typical Robert Frost poem. While the story is utterly realistic — in fact, Anand has told me that it is based upon his own childhood experience — it has an obviously symbolic dimension too. This is suggested by the fact that neither the child nor its parents, nor any other character in the story has a name; they are evidently representative figures. The fair — the scene of the child's experience also does not have a specific local habitation. As all this indicates, the child in the story is 'father of the man', for in the fair of the world, one often covets many things and then the loss of a near and dear one suddenly makes all coveted prizes appear totally worthless. As Guru Nanak says, 'we are all children lost in the world fair'. The story has a neat and balanced structure and the descriptions in a lyrical vein in the earlier half effectively bring out the moods of wonder and joy the child feels until the final blow falls.

Economy, brevity and a rich poetic vein characterise the story, *Lullaby* in an equal measure. Exhibiting a rare delicacy of touch, this is a fine evocation of a young working mother's state of mind as she sits rocking her dying child in her lap and recalling memories of her lover, while she feeds the machine with handfuls of jute, in a factory. Her persistent lullaby, 'Sleep/Oh sleep/My baby, sleep' has for its background music all the harsh sounds in the factory: 'the engine chuk-chuked; the leather belt khup-khupped; the bolts jig-jigged; the plugs tik-tikked'. Both the human song and the machine jazz are repeated in the story, and no sensitive reader will miss the telltale symbolic significance of the fact that at the end, the lullaby stops when the child dies, but the machine jazz goes on uninterrupted. The machine has ultimately triumphed over the human being, heedless of human hopes and frustrations.

Birth sows another working mother in a crisis, but this time far more fortunate in the upshot of her ordeal. Parvati, a poor peasant woman in an advanced state of pregnancy, is compelled to work at breaking stones, owing to the straitened circumstances of the family. The birth-pangs start as she is proceeding to her work alone; but, in this hour of trial she refuses to panic. Her native, rustic ruggedness is reinforced by an inner strength derived from her deep-seated, simple peasant faith in the gods. As she lies writhing on the ground, she sees a vision of Goddess Kali in the sky above. This gives her so much courage that when the child arrives she is even able to manage the necessary midwifery herself, and at the end, we find her putting the baby in the basket and going to break stones again. Like Gauri in Anand's novel, *The Old Woman and the Cow,* Parvati too is sustained by her traditional faith in her hour of need. The imaginative description of Parvati's ordeal lifts the entire narrative to a higher plane where the supernatural touch of her vision of Kali blends harmoniously with the emotionally charged atmosphere. Apart from this, the story also demonstrates how Anand's best work reveals a deep apprehension of what is enduring in the Indian folk tradition. Parvati is a representative figure; she is traditional rustic Indian womanhood at its very best.

A different mood characterizes *A Village Idyll,* a story most appropriately entitled. The imaginative opening, 'splashes of red and orange mingle into an aura of burning gold and, in a flash, the sun rises over the rim of the village pond, resplendent' sets the tone of this delightful picture of youthful love in a rural setting. While the 'manure cart', the 'lentil field' and the 'hay barn' make the story rooted in native soil, Govind and Gauri are more than rustic lovers. The lyrical descriptions make them archetypes of love: 'There is the voice of Siva in their curly throats. And in their bodies is the sinuous disunion of a broken moment between the lord of storms and his consort, Parvati. And in their touching is the burning of several planets, the extinction of worlds.'

In the *Five Short Fables* and *Little Chicks,* the scene shifts form the human to the animal world, though these short narratives often have human life as their ultimate point of reference, in spite of the fact that the protagonists belong to the beast Kingdom. The fables, obviously modelled on the *Panchatantra* and Aesop, however, show a variety of treatment. *The Golden Cockerel* and *Little Chicks* are almost pure description with no inherent symbolism, though the first has a touch of humour in its account of the cock frustrated in a love-fray, and the second depicts with tenderness three little chickens as 'miracles of littleness' learning the rules of the art of survival. Each of the rest of the fables ends with an explicit moral, *a la* Aesop, with a difference, however. *The Butterfly* pin-points the pathos of the law of 'beauty vanishes, beauty passes', *The Peacock* is a sermon on vanity and humility, and *A Leaf in the Storm* underscores the necessity to have roots but not to get rooted in barren fields". These fables differ from those of Aesop, in that the hard, clear cut contours of allegory which are so characteristic of the latter are replaced in them by lyrical description steeped in symbolic overtones.

The second group of stories in this selection is of those the prevailing mood of which is the consciousness of the 'tears at the heart of things'. These stories are naturally allied to the brief tales of 'lyric awareness' but with a difference. The treatment here is in the main, not symbolic but realistic (though symbolic overtones do occur) and the emphasis is on bringing home to the reader the pathos of the plight of men and women crushed by forces too strong for them to fight against. *Lajwanti* is the story of a young, motherless rustic girl, whose husband is away at college. She finds herself an easy target of the amorous attentions of her lascivious, pock-marked brother-in-law; discovers to her horror that her mother-in-law connives at his doings; runs away to her father's house but is sent back; and, in the end, tries unsuccessfully to drown herself in a well. As she is fished out, her plaintive cry is, 'there is no way for me... I am... condemned to live'. The caged *maina* which she carries with her in her flight, is evidently symbolic of her own situation, but the stark realism of her plight is unmistakable. Equally realistic is the portayal in *The Parrot in the Cage* of Rukmani, an old woman who has lost her all in the holocaust of the partition of India and whose sole companion during the migration from Lahore to Amritsar is a pet parrot. Like the *maina* in the previous story, the parrot here carries a symbolic suggestion; it perhaps shows how the old woman's deprivation is so total that her nearest and dearest now is not a human being but a bird. *The Gold Watch* presents an Indian clerk working in a British firm, who is forced to retire prematurely because a better connected replacement has been found for the job. On his retirement, he receives from his British boss a gold watch which he drops and breaks while receiving. The little mishap is symbolic of all that has gone wrong in the twenty-year long relationship between Sharma and his British superiors, with the Indian's pathetic inferiority complex being complemented by the white man's superiority complex. The breaking of the watch is perhaps also symbolic (like the shattering of Quentin's watch in *The Sound and the Fury*) on the protagonist's unconscious desire that time should stop, so that the future so painful to contemplate, should never materialize. *Old Bapu* and *The Cobbler and the Machine* are stories of two aged outcastes. Bapu, a weakling with a shrivelled leg has been deprived of his land by his uncle; he comes to a city in search of a livelihood, but since he looks as old as seventy (while he is only fifty), he cannot find work and is condemned to starve. Cobbler Saudagar's problem is the exact opposite one; it is over-work that kills him. The machine is his *La Belle Dame Sans merci.* Lured by it into contracting a huge debt', and soon, 'drained of his life-blood by the sweat that was always pouring off his body, he fell stone-dead one evening'.

These tales of pathos are also full of overtones of social criticism. Lajwanti's tale is representative of the helplessness of the Indian woman in the traditional rustic joint family. Rukmani's tale is typical of countless similar tragedies which were the legacy of the partition of India. *The Gold Watch,* as already suggested, is a revealing comment on race-relations; and while old Bapu's plight is a slap in the face of an economy which denies the citizen the fundamental right to work, *The Cobbler and the Machine* can also be regarded as a perceptive gloss on the seamy side of industrialism. Nevertheless, the dominant impression produced by these stories is not that of social criticism which remains subordinated to the pathos of the situation of the protagonists.

This strain of social awareness is central to the group of stories led by *The Power of Darkness.* In these tales, Anand's acute understanding of the complex social forces at work in modern India of today is a battle-ground where tradition clashes with modernity. When a huge dam is being expeditiously constructed in the Punjab, a little hamlet named after Goddess Kamli is about to be submerged. The villagers with their deep-rooted suspicions about anything modern consider the 'giant monster of cement and steel' as an insult to the goddess, and pertinently ask: How can your electricity vie with Kamli, the Mother? When this confrontation between obstinate orthodoxy and impatient modernity leads to an impasse, Bali provides a happy solution by a virtual stroke of genius. An electrician, who can also play the role of the village bard, Bali is himself an excellent example of a synthesis of the old and the new. By means of a rousing bardic recital he convinces the villagers that the very goddess who had incarnated herself in their village as Kamli, has now re-incarnated herself as electricity in the new dam.

In *The Tractor and the Corn Goddess* a similar problem is tackled but a different solution is indicated. The arrival of a tractor brought by a progressive minded young landlord creates panic in a village. The giant machine is severally accused of having desecrated Mother Earth: of violating the Corn Goddess; of containing jinns, bhuts and Shiv-Shakti of being a weapon of destruction with concealed guns to be used to shoot the peasants down. The clever landlord then has the tractor dismantled in the presence of the villagers, who are finally convinced that the thing is after all only so much of 'iron and steel, so tempered as to plough the land quickly'. The peasant's down-to-earth commonsense ultimately triumphs over superstition. The story is also a satire on the weight of convention in a feudalistic society. When the radical young landlord, who has newly succeeded to the estate, remits taxes and refuses to accept *nazrana,* his tenants, instead of being delighted are shocked at this lapse from feudalistic propriety.

Feudalism is also the object of Anand's satire in *A Kashmir Idyll* with its most ironic title. Here, what starts as a pleasure trip in Kashmir ends as a tragedy of feudal exploitation and retribution. A petty State nobleman compels young tenant to row his pleasure-boat, ignores the poor man's pitiful plea that he has to attend to the funeral of his mother who is just dead. The protesting young tenant is however, himself shocked at having annoyed his lord and master by so gross an act of disobedience, and grovels in the dust, in atonement. The fat Nawab, driven to hysterical glee at this conclusive demonstration of his feudal power is choked to death by his fit of laughter. The theme of how unjustly the haves treat the have-nots is handled in a more restrained manner in *The Price of Bananas,* in which a well-to-do businessman not only makes niggardly recompense for a service done to him by a fruit-vendor but also unjustly accuses him of having a hand in his discomfiture.

In all these stories of social criticism there is a clear under current of comedy (which in *A Kashmir Idyll* is mixed with a touch of the macabre). The ignorance of the village in *The Power of Darkness* and *The Tractor and the Corn Goddess* and the discomfiture of the rich businessman at the hands of the monkey in *The price of Bananas* are obviously diverting; but the comedy here is evidently secondary to satire on social mores. In *A pair of Mustachio, The Signature* and *Two Lady Rams* however, comedy holds the stage, relegating social criticism to the background, while in *The Liar* we have unalloyed laughter. *A Pair of Mustachios,* presents Khan Azam Khan, who claims descent from an ancient noble Afghan family. Now reduced to poverty, he still retains all his feudal hauteur of which his up-turned 'tiger mustache' is a concrete symbol. When he finds the village shopkeeper turning the tips of his mustaches upward until they resemble the aristocratic 'tiger mustache', he is so profoundly disturbed that he enters into a strange deal with the low-born shopkeeper, according to which, the Khan will transfer all his household goods and chattels to the *banya* on condition that both the tips of the mustaches of the upstart come down permanently and are kept glued in the 'Goat style' appropriate to his station in life. For the feudal 'downstart', the world is indeed well lost for a bunch of hair on the upper lip of an upstart. Feudalism is equally the source of farcical humour in *the Signature.* Subramaniam, a bank official who arrives at Aliabad to take the signature of the Nawab on an important document, finds a business which should normally take not more then a couple of minutes dragging for days together, since feudal etiquette demands that a guest be properly and elaborately entertained before any business is transacted. It is difficult to decide which is the more comic of the two-Subramaniam's plight in the feudal world in which he finds himself 'a stranger and afraid' or the Nawab's refusal to realise the futility of obstinately clinging to traditional feudal ways in the modern age.

The comedy in *Two Lady Rams* arises out of the complications of bigamy which, in the pre-Independence days in India was far from uncommon. Lalla Jhinda Ram receives a knighthood, the glory and joy of which are clouded by the fact that he has two wives (the first fifty and the second half her age) and each insists on attending the investiture ceremony as Lady Ram. He finally cuts the ceremony where the appearance of the two Lady Rams creates quite a sensation.

The Liar is a highly diverting account of Labhu, an old village *Shikari* whose tall tale of shikar are garnished with monsters, magicians and damsels.

The last three stories in this *selection — The Tamarind Tree, The Silver Bangles* and *The Thief* have one feature in common. They are all primarily studies in human psychology, though other elements such as social criticism, and humanitarian compassion, which are almost ubiquitous in Anand's work are also present in them. *In The Tamarind Tree, Roopa,* a young wife and an expectant mother cannot satisfy her longing to eat tamarind from her neighbour's tree, but a far greater disappointment for her is the sad realisation that the fear of the elders and the weight of convention have made it impossible for her to communicate satisfactorily with her husband, for her plight is that 'her inner impulses had always remained where they were, incommunicable even to her man.' This invests the story with obvious psychological interest, though ostensibly Roopa's tale would appear to be another variation on Anand's favorite theme viz., the position of woman in traditional Hindu Society.

In a similar way, superficially viewed, *The Silver Bangles* would appear to be a story on the usual theme of caste distinctions, but on closer scrutiny, is revealed to be a study in sexual jealousy. Here, a good-looking sweeper girl, who sports the silver bangles given to her on the occasion of her betrothal by her mother, is unjustly accused by the lady of the house, of having stolen them. The poor girl is also admonished that 'untouchables in the South are not supposed to wear silver at all'. As the ending of the story makes clear, the high caste lady of the house, who is sexually frigid, is actually jealous of the attraction her husband feels for the sweeper girl, and is only seeking refuge in her caste-superiority to hide her inferiority *vis-a-vis* the untouchable beauty.

The Thief, the last story in this group, is also far more than a presentation of the theme of humanitarian compassion as it would at first sight appear to be. Ganesh Prashad, the young protagonist in the story, feels a strange and irresistible sexual attraction for a dirty beggar woman and comes to realise that the source of this strange passion lies in an incident in the past when he had been responsible for the beating up of an innocent beggar whom he had unjustly accused of theft; 'and now, this hangover of an unkind act against one beggar had become an undertone beneath the lust for another'. This is perhaps a strange but by no means inappropriate kind of atonement for a deep-seated feeling of guilt which lies buried in the sub-conscious mind of the protagonist.

The range and variety of Anand's short stories are evinced not only in mood, tone and spirit but also in locale, characters and form. The setting ranges from the Punjab (as in *The Parrot in the Cage*) to Uttar Pradesh (as in *The Price of Bananas*) and Kashmir (as in *Kashmir Idyll*); and both the village and the city get almost equal representation. The men, women and children that move through these narratives come form different strata of society. A seedy-looking nobleman rubs shoulders here with an ambitious upstart; a timorous native clerk cringes before his British boss; a lost child searches frantically for its parents, and an old refugee woman hopes to make a new start in life. There is a virtual mine of human nature here. Anand's characters are almost always representative of men and women. Old Bapu, Srijut Sudarshan Sharma (in *The Gold Watch*), Khan Azam Khan (in *A pair of Mustachios*) and other men in Anand's stories are typical of the social milieu from which they come; and the same may be said of Anand's women characters — Phalini (in *Lullaby*), Parvati (in *Birth*) Lajwanti, and others.

Except in the *Fables*, the narrative element is always strong in Anand's short stories. He is a skilled story-teller who can usually tell an absorbing narrative, beginning close to the action as in *The Lair, The Silver Bangles* and *The Two Lady Rams,* or with short, apt description which creates the proper atmosphere as in *The Tamarind Tree, Birth* and *Lajwanti.* Occasionally, however, he *is* tempted to begin his stories in too leisurely a fashion, with a long introduction which delays the action unnecessarily. This is seen in stories like *The price of Bananas* and *The Signature,* though the long, leisurely introduction to *The power of Darkness* is perhaps a calculated device underscoring the bardic nature of the entire narrative. Most of

Anand's stories maintain their narrative thrust throughout, *A Kashmir Idyll* with its long, tourist guide type of place descriptions being an occasional exception. The endings of the stories show interesting variations. The action reaches a clinching conclusion in stories like *The Lost Child;* and *Lajwanti,* while in *The Thief* there is a fresh twist given to the action at the end, *a la* O' Henry *Birth* rightly ends on a note of hope for the future, and some of the *Fables,* not inappropriately, with a moral. Lullaby ends effectively with a refrain describing the factory scene and while there is a genuine poetic note here arising naturally out of the mood and tone of the narrative, the ending of *Silver Bangles* (Sajani lifted her head as a dove updives off the earth...) is open to the charge of poetizing, since the drift of the entire narrative does not support a conclusion in this vein, which strikes an obviously false note.

Like almost every other major Indian writer writing in English, Anand has given some thought to the problem of the use of the English language by an Indian for creative purposes. He has made a useful distinction between 'the higgledy-piggledy spoken English in our country' and 'the imaginative use of the same language in the hands of the creative writers in Indian English."[6] The former is 'Pidgin-English', and the latter he describes metaphorically as 'Pigeon-Indian', in which 'the words soar in the imagination like pigeon,' in flight.'[7] Analysing 'Pigeon-Indian', he says:

The psychology of Indian English is rooted in the Indian metabolism. Most Indians, who speak or write English, even

---

6 M.R. Anand, *'Pigeon-Indian: Some Notes on Indian English Writing', Journal of the* Karnataka University *(Humanities),* XVI, 1972, p. 72.

7 Ibid., p. 90

when they have been to Oxford and Cambridge... tend, naturally, to bring the hangover of the mother-tongue, spoken in early childhood into their expression... the pull of our mother-tongue leads to a heavy sugarcoating of ordinary English words. [8]

Regarding the creative process involved in his own writing, Anand declares:

I found, while writing spontaneously, that I was always translating dialogue *from* the original Punjabi into English. The way in which my mother said something in a dialect of central Punjab could not have been expressed in any other way except in an almost literal translation, which might carryover the sound and sense of the original speech. I also found that I was dreaming or thinking or brooding about two-thirds of the prose-narrative in Punjabi or in Hindustani, and only one-third in the English language;[9]

True to his creed, Anand's style almost aggressively sports peculiarities which make the Indian origins of his English unmistakably apparent. Colourful Indianisms permeate diction, idiom and imagery in the dialogue. Anand employs in his fictions expletives like' Acha,' 'ohe', 'wah', 'jaja', 'areray', honorifics such as 'huzoor', 'sardar', 'Maharaja' preserver of the poor' and 'sahib' while these are the authentic article, the use of ('sire' in *A Kashmir Idyll* and *The Power of Darkness* is clearly seen to strike a foreign and therefore false note); words used in a complimentary sense in a peculiar Indian fashion, such as 'they' and 'their' used by a wife while referring to her

8 Ibid., p. 78,

9 M.R. Anand, *Pigeon-Indian: Some Notes on Indian English Writing, Journal of the* Karnataka university *(Humanities)*, XVI, 1972, p. 81.

husband, and phrases hallowed by custom such as 'the wife of my son' as a form of address while talking to a daughter-in-law; terms of endearment such as 'My life'; colourful swear-words and imprecations reeking of the soil, as for instance, 'budmash', 'sala,' 'rape-mother', 'seed of a donkey' and 'eater of you masters'. (The use of the phrase 'sun of a gun' in "*The Tractor* and *the Corn, Goddess*" is a jarring exception) and Indian vernacular idiom literally translated into English as in 'Don't stand on my head', 'there is something black in the pulse', and 'Darkness has descended over the earth'.

Anand's English in the narrative portions, though correct and idiomatic on the whole, also shows distinct peculiarities which make its Indian origin clear viz., its oriental opulence, its passion for adjectives, its tendency to use more words than are absolutely necessary, and its fast, galloping tempo. Thus, Roopa in *The Tamarind Tree* has her nose 'bedewed... with jewels of perspiration'; 'little virulets of sweat trickle' through deep fissures of old age' which line Rukmani's face in *The Parrot in the Cage;* the agitation of old Bapu's nerves produces 'the aberration of a phantasma, like the red stars over a toothache'; and Lajwanti finds that 'Destiny spread(s) the length of dumb distance before her', and 'descending into the pit of confusion', she is 'lost in the primal jungle of turmoil'. Though this kind of stylistic opulence is almost overpowering for modern taste, it is a moot point whether it is not, in a way, typical of the Indian ethos shaped over centuries by the ornate utterances of Sanskrit and Persian literary modes. It would be as unreasonable to expect Anand to write like Hemingway, as it would have been to expect Faulkner to write like Maugham. Of course, there are occasions when Anand's quick flow of words and dense accumulation of conceits are not justified by his immediate subject. This would perhaps indicate an occasional failure of sensibility,[10] and sometimes a rather simplistic reading of life, though, at his best, as in *The Lost Child, Birth and Lullaby,* he does unmistakably show himself capable of looking into the heart of life.

With all this limitations, Anand's contribution to the Indian short story is truly impressive. He is a born story-teller, who has, at the same time thought deeply over his craft, drawing upon several sources in shaping it. He has an unerring sense of situation and a sure ability to visualize a sense clearly. His stories are a museum of human nature, and have a wide range and ample variety of mood and tone. Among the Indian short story writers in English, he has few peers.

---

10 In answer to this criticism that there is 'an occasional failure of sensibility', in a personal letter to me, the author writes: "In the ultimate analysis, my efforts at expressionism in the short story result here and there, in the diffusion of the metaphor, which inspires the tales — the love which connects all creatures, which I wish to infuse into my fiction in the face of the human situation. And, perhaps, some of my characters live in a kind of haze, with which I had intended to cover my sentiments. In the short stories about 'tears at the heart of the things', the elegy of *Lajwanti* may have remained a private lament. But *Old Bapu* is part of the vast tragedy, when he sees his face in the mirror and realises that he has grown old and is nearing death. In the stories of man's fate, baulked by the new cash-nexus society, happiness my be coloured by my over-enthusiasm to transform old gods into new gods and it is possible that the naive bard in *Power of Darkness* remains a silhouette. In *The Cobbler and the Machine,* however, Saudagar is realised. In the farcical tales, there is an inevitable resort to one-dimensional characters, like the Pathan in *A Pair of Mustachios.* In the stories about women and children, you will notice that the sensibility is sought to be ultimately fused, as in the pangs of Parvati in *Birth,* the anguish against the over-all fate as in *Lullaby* and the lostness of all the people in the world fair as in the *Lost Child.* In these tales you concede that I may have touched the heart of things."

Part I

'LYRIC AWARENESS'

I

The Lost Child*

It was the festival of spring. From the wintry shades of narrow lanes and alleys emerged a gaily clad humanity, thick as a swarm of bright-coloured rabbits issuing from a warren. They entered the flooded sea of sparkling silver sunshine outside the city gates and sped towards the fair. Some walked, some rode on horses, others sat, being carried in bamboo and bullock carts. One little boy ran between his parent's legs, brimming over with life and laughter. The joyous morning gave greetings and unashamed invitations to all to come away into the fields, full of flowers and songs.

"Come, child, come," called his parents, as he lagged behind, fascinated by the toys in the shops that lined the way.

He hurried towards his parents, his feet obedient to their call, his eyes still lingering on the receding toys. As he came to where they had stopped to wait for him he could not suppress the desire of his heart, even though he well knew the old, cold stare of refusal in their eyes.

"I want that toy," he pleaded.

---

* From *The Lost Child and Other Stories.*

His father looked at him red-eyed in his familiar tyrant's way. His mother, melted by the free spirit of the day, was tender, and giving him her finger to catch, said: 'Look, child, what is before you.'

The faint disgust of the child's unfulfilled desire had hardly been quelled in the heavy, pouting sob of a breath, 'm-o-th-er,' when the pleasure of what was before him filled his eager eye. They had left the dusty road on which they had walked so far. It wended its weary way circuitously to the north. They had come upon a footpath in a field.

It was a flowering mustard field, pale like melting gold as it swept across miles and miles of even land — a river of yellow liquid light, ebbing and falling with each fresh eddy of wild wind, and straying in places into broad rich tributary streams, yet running in a constant sunny sweep towards the distant mirage of an ocean of silver light. Where it ended, on one side stood a cluster of low mud-walled houses, thrown into relief by a dense crowd of yellow-robed men and women from which arose a high-pitched sequence of whistling, creaking, squeaking, roaring, humming noises, sweeping across the groves to the blue-throated sky like the weird, strange sound of Siva's mad laughter.

The child looked up to his father and mother, saturated with the shrill joy and wonder of this vast glory, and feeling that they, too, wore the evidence of this pure delight in their faces, he left the footpath and plunged headlong into the field, prancing like a young colt, his small feet timing with the fitful gusts of wind that came rich with the fragrance of more distant fields.

A group of dragon-flies were bustling about on their

gaudy purple wings, intercepting the flight of a lone black butterfly in search of sweetness from the flowers. The child followed them in the air with his gaze, till one of the them would fold its wings and rest, and he would try to catch it. But it would go fluttering, flapping, up into the air, when he had almost caught it in his hands. One bold black bee, having evaded capture, sought to tempt him by whining round his ear and nearly settled on his lips, when his mother gave a cautionary call: "Come, child, come, come on to the footpath."

He ran towards his parents gaily and walked abreast of them for a while, being, however, soon left behind, attracted by the little insects and worms along the footpath that were teeming out from their hiding-places to enjoy the sunshine.

"Come, child, come," his parents called from the shade of a grove where they had seated themselves on the edge of a well. He ran towards them.

An old banyan tree outstretched its powerful arms over the blossoming jack and jaman and neem and champak and scrisha and cast its shadows across beds of golden cassis and crimson gulmohur as an old grandmother spreads her skirts over her young ones. But the blushing blossoms freely offered their adoration to the Sun in spite of their protecting chaperon, by half covering themselves, and the sweet perfume of their pollen mingled with the soft, cool breeze that came and went in little puffs, only to be wafted aloft by a stronger breeze.

A shower of young flowers fell upon the child as he entered the grove and, forgetting his parents, he began to gather the raining petals in his hands. But lo! he heard the cooing of the doves and ran towards his parents, shouting:

"the dove! The dove!" The raining petals dropped from his forgotten hands. A curious look was in his parents' faces till a koel struck out a note of love and released their pent-up souls.

"Come, child come!" they called to the child, who had now gone running in wild capers round the banyan tree, and gathering him up they took the narrow, winding footpath which led to the fair through the mustard fields.

As they neared the village the child could see many other footpaths full of throngs, converging to the whirlpool of the fair, and felt at once repelled and fascinated by the confusion of the world he was entering.

A sweetmeat seller hawked: 'Gulab-jamun, rasgula, burfi, jalebi', at the corner of the entrance, and a crowd pressed round his counter at the foot of an architecture of many-coloured sweets, decorated with leaves of silver and gold. The child stared open-eyed and his mouth watered for the burfi that was his favourite sweet. "I want that burfi," he slowly murmured. But he half knew as he begged that his plea would not be heeded because his parents would say he was greedy. So without waiting for an answer he moved on.

A flower-seller hawked: 'A garland of gulmohur, a garland of gulmohur.' The child seemed irresistibly drawn by the implacable sweetness of the scents that came floating on the wings of the languid air. He went towards the basket where the flowers were heaped and half murmured, "I want that garland." But he well knew his parents would refuse to buy him those flowers because they would say they were cheap. So without waiting for an answer he moved on.

A man stood holding a pole with yellow, red, green and

purple balloons flying from it. The child was simply carried away by the rainbow glory of the silken colours and he was possessed by an overwhelming desire to possess them all. But he well knew his parents would never buy him the balloons because they would say he was too old to play with such toys. So he walked on farther.

A snake-charmer stood playing a flute to a snake which coiled itself in a basket, its head raised in a graceful bend like the neck of a swan, while the music stole into its invisible ears like the gentle rippling of a miniature waterfall. The child went towards the snake-charmer. But knowing his parents had forbidden him to hear such coarse music as the snake-charmer played, he proceeded farther.

There was a roundabout in full swing. Men, women and children, carried away in a whirling motion, shrieked and cried with his dizzy laughter. The child watched them intently going round and round, a pink blush of a smile on his face, his eyes rippling with the same movement, his lips parted in amazement, till he felt that he himself was being carried round. The ring seemed to go fiercely at first, then gradually it began to move less fast. Presently the child, rapt, finger in his mouth beheld it stop. This time, before his overpowering lover for the anticipated sensation of movement had been chilled by the thought of his parents' eternal denial, he made a bold request: 'I want to go on the roundabout, please, father, mother.'

There was no reply. He turned to look at his parents. They were not there ahead of him. He turned to look on either side. They were not there. He looked behind. There was no sign of them.

A full deep cry rose within his dry throat and with a sudden jerk of his body he ran from where he stood, crying in real fear, 'Mother father!' Tears rolled down from his eyes, hot and fierce; his flushed face was convulsed with fear. Panic-stricken, he ran to one side first, then to the other, hither and thither in all directions, knowing not where to go. "Mother, father!" he wailed with a moist, shrill breath now, his throat being wet with swallowing the spittle. His yellow turban untied and his clothes, wet with perspiration, became muddy where the dust had mixed with the sweat the dust had mixed with the sweat of his body. His light frame seemed heavy as a mass of lead.

Having run to and fro in a rage of running for a while he stood defeated, his cries suppressed into sobs. At little distances on the green grass he could see, through his filmy eyes, men-and women talking. He tried to look intently among the patches of bright yellow clothes, but there was no sign of his father and mother among these people, who seemed to laugh and talk just for the sake of laughing and talking.

He ran quickly again, this time to a shrine to which people seemed to be crowding. Every little inch of space here was congested with men but he ran through people's legs, his little sob lingering "Mother, father!" Near the entrance to the temple, however, the crowd became very thick men jostled each other, heavy men, with flashing, murderous eyes and hefty shoulders. The poor child struggled to thrust a way between their feet but, knocked to and fro by their brutal movements, he might have been trampled underfoot had he not shrieked at the highest pitch of this voice: "Father, mother!" A man in the surging crowd heard his cry and, stooping with very great difficulty, lifted him up in his arms.

"How did you get here, child? whose baby are you?" the man asked as he steered clear of the mass. The child wept more bitterly then ever now and only cried: "I want my mother, I want my father!"

The man tried to soothe him by taking him to the roundabout. "Will you have a ride on the horse?" he gently asked as he approached the ring. The child's throat tore into a thousand shrill sobs and he only shouted: "I want my mother, I want my father!"

The man headed towards the place where the snake-charmer still played on the flute to the swaying cobra. "Listen to that nice music, child" he pleaded. But the child shut his ears with his fingers and shouted his double-pitched strain: "I want my mother, I want my father!" The man took him near the balloons, thinking the bright colours of the balloons would distract the child's attention and quieten him. "Would you like a rainbow-coloured balloon?" he persuasively asked. The child turned his eyes from the flying balloons and just sobbed: "I want my mother, I want my father."

The man, still importunate in his kindly desire to make the child happy, bore him to the gate where the flower-seller sat. "Look! can you smell those nice flowers, child? Would you like a garland to put round your neck?" The child turned his nose away from the basket and reiterated his sob: "I want my mother, I want my father."

Thinking to humour his disconsolate charge by a gift of sweets, the man took him to the counter of sweet shop. "What sweets would you like, child?" he asked. The child turned his face from the sweet shop and only sobbed: "I want my mother, I want my father."

2

Lullaby*

'SLEEP
Oh sleep
My baby, sleep,
Oh, do not weep,
sleep
Like a fairy...'

sang Phalini as she rocked her little one-year old Suraj Mukhi in her lap while she fed the machine with handfuls of jute.

Would he ever get to sleep?

'sleep
Oh, sleep
My baby, sleep...'

His flesh was so warm. She could feel the heat of his little limbs on her thighs, a burning heat which was mixed with a sour smell. He must be ill. All day he had not shut his eyes, all day he had sobbed and cried.

The engine chuk-chuked; the leather belt khupp-khupped;

* From *The Barber's Trade Union and Other Stories.*

the bolts jig-jigged; the plugs tik-tikked; the whole floor shook like the hard wooden seat of a railway train.

And she had to go on feeding the gaping mouth of the machine. 'Bap re bap, why is this bitch barking?' the sharp-tongued women who sang folk-songs, and could brook no one else singing, called to the other women.

'sleep,
Oh, sleep...'

Phalini felt her throat growing hoarse with the jute fluff she had been swallowing since she had let the fold of the apron rag, with which she ordinarily padded her mouth and nose in the factory, fall loose. The fluff seemed to be everywhere — on the walls, over the machine, on her face. She could feel it streaming down her nose, her cheeks, to the silver ring round her neck which was green with sweat. She cast her eyes over her nose and felt how ugly it was as it stood out from her hollow cheeks. That is why she had pawned her big silver nose-ring which her mother-in-law had given her in the dowry, and refused to adorn her nostrils even though it was a bad omen to take off your jewellery.

'Ooon...ooon...ooon,...' Suraj Mukhi cried. The sharp, feeble cry stirred the black night of Phalini's soul as the air stirs the water but the child's voice was drowned in the dithyrambic hum of the preparing-shed in the factory.

'sleep
Oh, sleep
My baby, sleep,
Oh, do not weep,
Sleep,'

she sang, bending over the child's head till she almost touched the feverish brow and kissed the close-fisted hands which Suraj Mukhi was rubbing on his eyes even as he cried. And then she threw another handful of jute into the jaws of the monster.

Her own voice sounded to her like the whisper of a broken reed, completely out of tune today, as it had seldom been out of tune when she sang the work song:

'Roller Roll
Spread jute
Open mouth,
Rise jute
Fall seeds,
Work into cloth.'

Her big troubled eyes roved away from the child to the gaping mouth of the machine, beyond the black, greasy bolts and knobs and pistons, above the fumes of the thick, sickly, tasteless air in the shed.

The engine chuk-chuked; the leather belt khupp-khupped; the bolts jig-jigged; the plugs tik-tikked; the whole floor shook like the hard wooden seat of a railway train.

She felt giddy.

She had felt like that five months before she had given birth to a child: and oily taste in the mouth with a bile under the tongue that seemed to go quivering into the swollen pitcher of her belly and bring the entrails up to her throat. But the quickening under her navel and the memory of her lover's face seemed to offset the nausea. She tried to think of him now, as he had looked when he first came down from the Northern hills.

The wild, waspish boy with large brown eyes which had flashed when he had talked to her husband, Kirodhar, but which were so shy when he looked at her. Suraj Mukhi's eyes were like his. Also Suraj Mukhi's limbs smelt like his. But he would never know that he was the father of her child. Why, he was a child himself. He had come like lightening and gone like the thunder of the Northern hills...

Where had he gone, she wondered. Had he only come to give her the pang of parting? Where had he gone? It was now summer again and he was here last summer. For days she had scanned the horizon of the sky above the city, towards the north in the direction where he had gone. But he didn't seem to be any where" in the large breathless space. Only Suraj Mukhi lay in her arms. And the sun, after which she had named the child, stood high. And the tears rolled down her scalded face to her chin, across her cheeks, before she realised that she was weeping... Oh, where was he, the gay child, her lover, her baby, so simple, so stubborn, so strong?

'And I shall grow old and grief, not Kirodhar, shall be my Lord...'

'Oom...Ooom...' the child moaned.

The engine chuk-chuked; the leather belt khupp-khupped; the bolts jig-jigged; the plugs tik-tikked; the whole floor shook like the hard wooden seat of a railway train. And 'she had to go on feeding the mouth of the machine.

'Bap, re bap, what is the matter with the brat?

Can't you keep him quiet? said the women next to her.

Phalini saw him as she had seen him in a dream one day, standing by her side, smiling to her so that she had wanted to clasp him close to her breast. But she had stretched her arms towards him, she had suddenly wakened and found herself groping in the dark towards Kirodhar, who had thought she wanted him and had taken her. He must be somewhere in the far-off-hills, doing what? Wandering perhaps, happy and free, while she was caged here with her child.

She bent down to look at the child. His eyes were open, his face was still, he cried no more. That was good, she could feed the machine with more jute.

'Sleep
Oh, sleep
My baby, sleep...'

she sang, and she smiled at him and rocked him again.

Suraj Mukhi's eyes just stared at her; rigid and hard his little hand lay on the side.

She swayed on her haunches and left the jute.

The effigy lay still.

Dead.

She gave a long, piercing shriek which tore through the ceiling.

She slapped her cheeks and beat her palms on her breast, crying in a weird, hollow voice: 'Hai, hai.'

'Bap re bap, why is she crying, this bitch? What is the matter with her? Said the woman next to her.

'My child, my child, my child...' Phalini cried, crazed and agonized as she tore her hair.

The women crowded round her.

'What is the matter?' the forewoman called. 'Why are you bitches running amok?'

The engine chuk-chucked; the leather belt khupp-khupped; the bolts jig-jigged; the plugs tik-tikked; the whole floor shook like the hard wooden seat of a railway train...

3

Birth*

The Earth seemed to groan as Parvati heaved away from the busti in the hollow of the hills and her throat tightened in the breathless dark. The kikar trees on the road loomed like Jinns before her eyes, while the tremors in her belly drugged her with a dull pain as sweet as the scent of the Queen-of-the Night. Her father-in-law, who had been keeping at a respectable distance from her, was almost lost to view, except that she could hear his short, angry voice, now and then, beckoning her to hurry. And, in order to assure him that she was following, as also to assure herself against the frightening trees, she answered that she was following. But her feet were getting heavier and heavier this morning while her torso, in spite of the bundle on her head, pushed forward like the prow of a stately ship.

As she had started off in the early hours of the morning from the cluster of huts near Karole Bagh towards Ridge Road, where her husband had already gone to work, road mending, she had felt the child stirring in her belly. Perhaps it was turning over to take another, more comfortable position as

* From *The Tractor and the Corn Goddess and Other Storks.*

he had seemed to be doing all night. And she had put her hand on her belly ever so tenderly, as though to reassure the babe. And she had smiled the slightest wisp of a smile to think of what Ramu had done during the night and throughout the middle months of her pregnancy whenever she told him that the baby was stirring in her: he had put his ears on her stomach and listened and, then playfully tapping with his fingers, he would intone a crazy, humorous sing-song:

Patience, son, patience,

You must learn to be patient,

You must learn to cultivate the long-breasted-sense of your ancestors.

Now as she felt another stirring in her belly she superstitiously thought that it was probably Ramu's tricks which were responsible for the disturbance in her womb. For, not only had her husband been teasing her all the way form Ambala in the train, but he had had her until only a month ago in spurts of wild desire while her father-in-law was asleep in the hut.

She paused for a moment, balanced the bundle of food on her head with her left hand, while she stroked her belly with her right hand. The growing life in her swirled from side to side, so that her heart throbbed violently with fear and her head was dizzy with weakness. She gritted her teeth and clenched her hands to avoid fainting and, mercifully, the griping pain passed. She breathed hard and proceeded on her way.

The feeble echo of her father-in-law's voice fell on her ears: 'Oh hurry!'

She lifted her voice and answered back: 'I am following, Baba, I am following.'

And, all of a quiver at the momentary passing of pain, she was now anxious for the old man, sorry to be a burden on him who had really broken under the burden of responsibilities, specially when he had to mortgage his land and buy the fares to Delhi. And yet, throughout, he had been solicitous for her welfare, and that had always moved her. Actually, of course his concern was more for the son's son that she might bear for him than for her. But, nevertheless, his consideration was more touching because he was so child-like in his anxiety and so warm-hearted, in spite of the bad luck that had been pursuing him like a malevolent spirit all these years. For instance, he had refused to believe her mother-in-law when, lingering on her death-bed, she had maliciously attributed the decline of the whole family to the day when, five years ago, she Parvati had come to their house as Ramu's wedded wife. No, he had not believed the old woman and had scoffed at her even when the price of his disbelief in his wife's obsession was a protracted sulking on her part which hastened her death from cancer. And she, Parvati, had felt ever since that she must justify the old man's faith in her and give him a grandson, if only as a compensation for the loss of his wife and as the only happiness that might compensate him for the slow agony of his ruin through the debt and the drought.

Another tremor of pain, and the sickness of bile in the mouth...

But she gritted her teeth again and felt that she must hold out if only for the sake of appearances, because, earthy and natural as the old man was, he might be embarrassed if she gave birth to the child on the way to work. She must wait till her husband was near at hand and could fetch a woman from among the other stone-breakers to deliver her.

She hurried along, the tension in her nerves heightening under the layers of heat that oozed from the shadows of the lingering night. And beads of perspiration covered her nose and her forehead, and she felt as if she were choking for lack of breath. But she did not relax her hold on herself and, keeping her belly uplifted before her even as a drummer keeps a drum, her head held high, she strode along majestically forward.

For moments she could see herself walking along, almost as though she were the spectator of her own acts. Perhaps, it was from the nodal point of a strange apathy, which comes on to a pregnant woman, that she could see her soft advance, proud like that of a she-peacock, feeling upon feeling in her body spending itself into a silence which was somewhat like the death from which all life begins. Over her tendons spread the morasses of inertness, from which came the echoes of pain, dull thuds of the sound of her babe stirring, struggling, reaching out through the sheaths of liquid held up by the trauma of birth. And through this pent-up race between the elements in her belly, the vision of the dull whites of her eyes played havoc with the black points, so that each branch of a tree became the intricate coil of serpents from which hung the skulls of donkeys, stags, lions, elephants, monkeys side by side with the bodies of the damned humans in the orchards of hell.

There was the slightest whirr of fear at the back of her head as this image of an early legend about the trees in hell crept up behind the film of grit in her eyes. The sight of a white-washed grave, with a green flag on top of it, increased the fear and she shook a little. This caused a rumbling in her belly and sent sparks of shooting pain charging the quagmire of her mind, stirring the memories of terror built up through the talk of her mother. She was in the panic of a confusion and began to run, trying to hold her head erect and her torso suspended before her, as though she were guarding both the beauty of her gait as well as her unborn child against the shadows of the trees, against all the grisly populations which confronted her. The films on her startled eyes became thicker in the blind rush forward and her nostrils dilated like those of a young bay mare pursued by the devil. She opened her mouth to shout for her father-in-law, but though her lips were agape no sound came out of them.

And now she tried to control herself, to banish the fear of the haunting shadows by an extroversion of will. And for a moment, she paused, her breasts heaving, her breath coming and going quickly, and the whole of her body bathed in a sweat. But now a spiral wave of weakness rose to her head and she felt giddy. Through her half-closed eyes, she could see her father-in-law like a speck of dust against the huge boulders of the Birla Temple on Ridge Road, outside which was the pitch where she was to go to break stones. If only she could survive this faint, she could make it and be out of the reach of these graves!... The opiate of heat and fatigue was on her numb body now, however, and, while she clenched her hands in readiness to advance, the pain in her abdomen became a growl like the noisy motion of the wheel on the road-making engine and she receded back into the arms of the *doots* of hell.

She stamped the earth, as though to beckon it, as Sita had

done asking it to open up and swallow her hour of peril. The earth did not open up, but she steadied a little. The pain in her belly was swirling in wild waves, round and round, up and down, the *aus* stirring in the cauldron of her belly, sizzling and boiling over.

Shaking her head in defiance of the demons both inside and outside her, holding her stomach in her left head, the corners of her tightly closed mouth twitching in a frenzy of desperation, her face wrinkled, she moved with a deliberate calm towards the hollow ditch which stretched by the road. And lowering the basket off her head, she fell back with a thud on to the hump of the ditch. Fortunately, she had landed on her yielding bottom.

For a while, she lay back and tried to rest herself, hoping that the spell of pain would pass. But as soon as she dosed her eyes shes felt the moisture between her loins and knew that her baby had started.

Slow ache of yearning, like the bursting desire for her man, blended with the rich smell of aus, and she felt as though she was in a dragged stupor, involved in a kind of ennui in which the nerves of her body seemed to relax. Her brows knitted into a frown, the corners of her lips tightened and her eyes contracted, there were pinpoints of sweat on her nose and a scowl on her face. She felt afraid that she might evaporate into nothingness, just pass out, a sagging heap of flesh dissolving under the pressure of the child in her belly.

She wanted to harden her mind so that she could save herself, but the mind is the body and the body mind, so that the will to power over her soul only rigidified her flesh; and she lay in a tense, unbending pose.

In moment, however, her ego dissolved under the impact of further waves of pain. And now she was gasping for breath, a helpless, grey bird, smothered by the overwhelming forces that rose from her belly, the powerful music of her distended entrails drowning her resistances through a series of involuntary shrieks.

'Oh god, oh my god!' she cried out.

And then, as though the invocation of the Deity had put her in touch with heaven from the drugged stupor of her brain, there arose glimpses of random visions, configurations formed by the specks of cloud on the blue sky. Beyond the haze of delirium in her eyes, there stood the picture of an enormous woman lying down flat. And it seemed to her as though this woman in the clouds was also in the travail of childbirth.

Suppressing her groans, urged by deep curiosity and the superstitious belief that heavenly powers often appear to help human beings in their time of trouble, she stared hard at the hulking form. The image seemed to change and get fixed before her in the shape of the Goddess Kali, recumbent in her benevolent mood by the side of the crouching God, Shiva. And she felt a sudden wave of resentment that her husband was not by her side, seated there, helping her. He had known that she was nearing her time. In fact, he had known it this morning because she had tossed about from side to side restlessly all night. And yet he had rushed off to work, leaving her to bear the pain all alone... Oh, if only, only... if she could touch a sympathetic hand, or limb — oh anything, if only she could clutch a straw to help while the excruciating pain gnawed at her entrails and twisted her from hip to hip...

But she turned her face away from the clouds in the sky and cursed herself for thinking ill of her husband, the lord and master whom her parents had married her off to and whom they expected her to worship. And then she thought of the joy she had had when he had come to her on the night that she conceived his child.

Senses emerging from indifference and the fatigue of the day's work like a rich perfume drugging her body into excitement. Aroused vitals urging her strong buttocks against the pressure of his body. Surging of warmth in her belly and under her breasts, even as there was this heat inside her now, melting of mouth to mouth... And then the soporific faintness in the head, not unlike the giddiness that possessed her in this childbirth. Sighing, eyes half closed, limbs taut, enraptured at the swirling of his maddening strokes, smothered...

She could recall the feelings of those moments with a strange clarity on the curve of her present pleasure and pain, she could sense in the spell of writings in her haunches the swelling and unswelling of passion. Only, the pain was gradually reducing her to pulp till her eyes were closing against her will and she was shrieking...

'Oh mother! Oh my mother!' she cried, panting for breath as though she was suspended between life and death. And, for a moment she lay back exhausted as though she could not go on with it.

Then, with clenched teeth and a deliberate intent to control the spreading panic in her limbs, she raised her head and set up in a crouching position.

Draggers of shooting pain seemed to plunge into her

sides as though each nerve had sharpened into steel. Crushing weight of centuries of anguish seemed to press on her belly. And there was the endless grain-grind of churning of the oceans inside her, the crushing of worlds over her head and the struggle of random elements, each shooting pain emerging out of the source of energy in her belly into a storm tossed outer universe. Perspiration simply poured down her face now and blended with the pressure of the elements that dug pinpoints of heat into her flesh.

'Oh, come, come, child come,' she cried out aloud almost like an incantation. 'Come, come, my babe,' she whispered even as she has breathed love words on the night that the seed was sown.

And she hardened her body so that the tenderness in her could be released, whipping her buttocks with her hands, striking the sides of waist, swaying to and fro, gritting her teeth and hissing till she felt her haunches sagging and her bones twisting, till she could see her frame being pulled by elemental forces which seemed to have come and taken possession of her, the opposite tensions arising from nothingness and swaying like a strange and heavy rhythm of the earth's primitive energies.

With a smile on her face, a grim smile, she held her head in her hands and lay back in the position in which she had first fallen. And, beckoning all the resources of her will, collecting the tension of her nerves in her clenched fists, she strained and heaved in a series of protracted efforts. The heavy smell of an extraordinary drowsiness sustained her as involuntary tears rolled down her cheeks and as she groaned. The twistings and turnings of her waist contorted her body into a strange amorphous shape. And, above the protuberance of her churning' stomach, her heart beat like the echo of all the throbbings of previous months...

At last after an hour of torment as she lay drenched in a pool of blood and aus, she felt a boundless surging overwhelm her.

And, with a twitch of horror which faded into a mute triumph, the child came with a thin little cry, a dark bundle of tender, wrinkled flesh, a boy breathing softly but tingling with warm life.

Clutching him with eager, deft hands, she performed the services of the midwife on herself with the cool, assured touch which only the old dai, Kesari, in her native village, was known to bring to her task. And, what was most surprising, even to her, was the fact that having cut the naval strings which united her child to her with the rough end of the silver hansli round her neck, she emptied the basket in which she carried the food, donated the roti to the birds as a gift-offering, put her baby in it and strode forth towards the Ridge to go and break stones.

The darkness of the twilight sky was crumbling and the early morning sun had brightened the sky. But, as Parvati approached the pitch where she worked, the other stone breakers could not recognise her, because she looked different with the basket in her arms rather than on her head as she usually carried it. When, however, she came and laid the whining child at their feet, they were breathless with wonder. 'A witch this Parvati!' an old woman said. 'to be sure, a demon!' a man remarked.

'To be sure!' added Ramu, her husband coming towards

the basket to have a look at his child.

'The Goddess helped me in my travail,' whispered Parvati. 'I saw her in the clouds...'

The women left their work and rushed towards her, some open mouthed, some with prayers and incantations on her lips.

'Stop all this *cain cain,* woman!.' shouted her father-in-law as he came up from where he had been tarring the road to look at his grandchild. 'Get away', he said with a bluff of rudeness. 'It is no wonder that she had the little one all by herself. She is a peasant woman with strong loins like many other peasant woman of our parts, who have given birth to sons all by themselves, so that our race can be' perpetuated and our land tilled for grain...' And he picked up the whining baby from the basket like a practised hand and put the little shrieking one to his shoulder, saying with a gruff tenderness: 'Come, come, my lion, my stalwart, don't weep... come, it won't be so bad. Come, my son, perhaps with your coming, our luck will turn...'

4

A Village Idyll*

Splashes of red and orange mingle into an aura of burning gold and, in a flash, the sun rises over the rim of the village pond, resplendent.

Gauri comes treading on the pearls of dew on the tufts of grass by the ditch to fetch water, with a pitcher under her arm.

'Oh, the fair one.

Oh, ripe like the juice of a sugarcane...'

Govind sighs, as he sits rubbing his clothes with soap on a slab of stone, 'the glow produced by the brisk movement on his face ripens into crimson and his breath almost fails.

Gauri shyly draws the end of her dupatta over her head and dips her pitcher in the water, but as she leans forward, the tips of her brave breasts are silhouetted against the sky line.

'May I be your sacrifice!' Govind whispers the familiar ejaculation of heart-squanderers in the streets of Verka. And, as though the words are potent like a magic spell, the blood rushes down from his head to his heart and loins, the centres

---

* From *The Tractor and the Corn Goddess and Other Stories.*

of storm in his peasant soul, 'Oh the fair one! he hisses. And the hisses splutter into an embarrassed cough.

At that Gauri laughs even as her pitcher gurgles with a series of hysterical reverbertions.

And with that their love started. For, in the tickling of her throat and the saliva on his tongue was the meeting of long distances, of uneasy colloquies, of thumping hearts and reckless yearning.

She stood before him, her breasts heaving towards the morning, her senses sinuously touching the edge of demure restraint, her blood warming and melting and leaping like flames towards a ceiling in a conflagration.

He stared at the wonder of her, his body taut, his breath swelling and unswelling to the tune of his now frightened heart, his soul reaching out to some expression from the groin of endless silence. She seemed like some shimmering cloud image, veiled in sheaths of innocence, 'Ha!' ... the exclamation escaped from his throat involuntarily. And he leapt towards her like a tiger towards a young doe.

With a shrill shriek she ran, leaving her pitcher where it stood at the edge of the pond. And, as she raced up the steep bank, her torso straining forward but her legs far behind, she knew she was defeated and burst into a smile.

Govind caught her and flung her on to a dune. She fought him back, digging her nails into him and kicking him with upraised knees. He swung her from side to side and pinned her arms to the earth and lay down on her.

'Oh, Let me go,' she said with tears in her eyes and

laughter in her mouth. The colour on his face called to the radiance on cheeks. And, giddy-eyed, she relaxed, till his lips touched hers. And now she swayed as though her soul was in a delirium of giving.

'Someone will see us,' she whispered.

But, storm tossed, scampering, wriggling hard twitching with the concentration of nerves outstretched for months in desire for her, in a fierce felicity, he was intent on the dissolution of her energies, the melting of the snows of her virginity...

A little distance away, on the track leading to the rivulet, Lehna, the son of the Landlord, went twisting the tails of his bullocks, goading them to drag the manure cart quicker. Govind flapped his arms like a protective male bird covering his mate under his wings for Lehna was his rival. Gauri snuggled up to him like a cooing female bird. And thus they lay in the heat and the sweat, their voices rustling like the silks of Lahore and their faces glowing about the dune sands like two luminous wild flowers jutting out of the earth. The sun shone above their heads.

The sun shines, and the moon takes light from it, as also the stars. And on the earth, going round the sun, through the eternal movements, we possess in our spines all the planets, as well as a thirsty love and the desire to die in order to be reborn... And from the dying, and through the rebirth, there grow lotuses among the reeds, the flaming smiling pinks, pushed up in the quagmire by the vital spark that keeps things alive. In the fruits, flowers, foliages among the birds, beasts and humans, the same glorious urge prospers. And thee is creation.

Gauri smiles like the demure morning. Govind laughs like the temple drum. There is the voice of Siva in their curly throats. And in their bodies is the sinuous disunion of a broken moment between the lord of storms and his consort, Parvati. And in their touching is the burning of several planets, the extinction of worlds, the smothering of heavens, the dissolution of hells, and the springing of a serene pleasure, muted like a prayer in which we rest, sometimes as before a new miracle and sometimes, as before the juxtaposition of legs interwined in a ridiculous posture.

And thus begins a cycle.

Govind met Gauri in the lentil field on the first full moon night of autumn when every one was awake and merry. He lay with her in a hay barn on the eighth day of the new moon before winter, when people were feasting at night after fasting the whole day. And he took her on every moon-lit night in the winter. For, after the first flush of raw passion had expended itself under the sun, they began more and more to lend themselves to the mellow light of the moon. Govind wore clean clothes and Gauri always had flowers in her hair.

As Gauri went to meet Govind in the fields by the river on one eclipse night, however, her mother saw her. 'Ah!' she shrieked at the boy, 'if you have spoiled my daughter, you must marry her... you wretch....' And she shrieked at Govind's mother for letting her son roam round like a bull. And Govind's mother shrieked at Govind's father for begetting a seducer. And Govind's father shouted at Govind. To which the boy returned the simple answer: 'Marry me to the girl.'

And then there was much toing and froing among the elders.

And at last, on an auspicious day, discovered in the scrolls of their fate, for a good commission by Pandit Badri Nath, the Brahmin priest, Govind and Gauri were married....

5

Five Short Fables*

THE DOVE AND THE CROW

Gliding softly through the clouds like a sunray on a grey morning, the dove descended towards her nest in the banyan tree. In her beak were tightly held two grains gathered from a nearby field, and in her eyes was a liquid light, almost like a squint, from the concentration of her desire to get home for her eggs.

As she reached within sight of the tree, she inclined on her shoulder, to the left, opened her wings wide and embraced the air, as though she was about to settle on the firmament. Her eyes were intent and her heart felt the pull of home. The light of the day shone across her neck like a smile.

Before her now stood the taller branches of the banyan tree. Only a little while ago had she ascended into the air from the cluster of leaves on the edge of the biggest branches of the banyan. But, somehow, the leaves seemed different, they seemed to have been parted from above.

---

* From *The Power of Darkness and Other Stories.*

The concentration of the light in the dove's eyes nearly tore the air, as she quickly wheeled and made an effort to dive into the pit for there was the sign, the sure sign, of the crow's approach towards her nest. And this crow was the sworn enemy of her eggs, the vandal, the destroyer, who had twice before killed her young ones just before they had been born. He always came from the top of the tree because he knew that her husband, the He-dove slept near the base of the tree in a little nest on a cavity of the main trunk.

She tore through as though her second sight, and her mother love, had combined to make her the vehicle of flight itself. And what looked like a nose dive became a safe landing on the top of the tree.

She sat on a strong twig, folded her wings and tried to collect herself together. A thin gauze of confusion covered her and her body trembled in spite of her will to remain calm. From what secret source of energy arose the passion, she knew not, but in her nerves, from deep beneath her flesh, there arose tremors which disturbed the even flow of her breath and the usual peace of her presence.

She cooed.

Immediately she heard the caw caw of her enemy, the crow, from below.

The ugly eater of dirt had surely destroyed her eggs. She fluttered and cooed.

The crow caw-cawed and was heard to hop away.

Collecting herself together, she peered into the pit below her and with the concentration of instinct, saw her nest. The two eggs she had been hatching lay, grey-white. Perhaps, they were safe. She had come in time.

There was no breath in her to wait. She darted to the branch on which, among the leaves, nestled her little home.

The crow cawed defiantly, even as he hopped a little way away from the branch.

Shivering through fear and trembling on the borders of hope, the mother dove walked to her nest. And, blind, but with her nerves taut, she spread her wings to feel the contours of her eggs beneath the warm down of her belly. Warm were the eggs beneath her safe, untouched. She had come in time, before the crow had attacked them. She cooed with satisfaction, with the instinct of the mother who finds her little ones safe after the agony of separation... She cooed deeply as she felt them near her flesh... She cooed again and spread her wings as though the little ones, still unhatched could listen...

The crow caw-cawed, even as he heard the dove coo. He wanted to frighten her, to bully her, as though to say: 'Your eggs are safe now, but I can still get them if I like; I have a strong beak, to fight with and my claws are strong like a vulture's.'

The mother dove cooed, this time a deep shriek of a coo, to call her husband, the sleepy lazy-bones, who had slept through the crisis, on the outpost in the cavity of the trunk of the banyan tree.

There was no answer.

She cooed again, more shrilly.

The crow caw-cawed to drown her soft voice.

She felt helpless. But the eggs were safe near the belly and she spread her wings wide and, looking this side and that, she sat, on the defensive, alert, equal to the fight, should he attack before the He-dove came.

The crow knew that he could not attack. He had lost his opportunity. Perhaps if the He-dove did not come he could overpower the mother dove and break her eggs, take her stock of grain and despoil her nest. Only, should the He-dove awake and call the other birds, together, his chance would be lost.

The dove cooed.

Stung by failure, craven and mad, the crow suddenly hopped nearer towards her to attack.

Fluttering, shrieking, cooing, with her wings spread wide, the grey mother dove stood on guard... And, nerved to resist, should the crow attack, she cooed defiantly, though a coo can never be a hoarse shout, as a caw can never be a whisper.

The little sparrows below heard the agonised coo of the mother dove. The He-dove awoke as the strange coo of mother dove fell into his ears. The little sparrows raised a hue and cry.

The mother dove cooed softly now, with assurance. The crow attacked her, picking at her wings in a desperate effort to avenge himself on her for her alertness. The dove fluttered wildly and beat of the attack, the white of her under-wings glistening like the light of danger before the cawing crow.

The He-dove flew up, followed by the sparrows. The crow caw-cawed and fled far to the end of the branch. The mother dove cooed to the He-dove, half remonstrating, half satisfied that he had come after all. The sparrows chirped and mocked at the crow.

The He-dove was stung by the reproach of the mother dove, cooed deeply and proudly, and lifted his beak towards the crow. The crow rubbed his beak with his feathers to clean it of the blood he had on it.

The mother dove cooed with pain. The He-dove came and put his beak into her beak. The kiss gave the mother dove warmth and she cooed with love. The crow fled away at the sound of the love song, cawing bitter hatred in his mouth.

They say in the Punjab that the dove can resist the attack of the crow, her proverbial enemy, with cooing. For the cooing comes from the deep, deep love of the mother for its young ones, and the cawing of the crow, as well as its red-eyed anger, comes from the smoke and ashes of the hatred in his heart.

THE BUTTERFLY

Pink, purple, mauve, scarlet, emerald and gold are the sweet peas on the bed at the end of the garden. And it seems the butterflies are like flying flowers, as their wings have all these colours on them. But the gay impropriety with which they flit from the pollen of one stem to the other, makes them transitory moments against the flowers, which will still be there through the autumn. That is why I feel an irresistible desire to catch a butterfly.

I sit, book in hand, trying to read, but the edges of my further eyes are captivated by one yellow meteor, with black dots, which intersects the triangle of the green expanse before me, somersaults, darts lightly forward and descends like a helicopter on a purple sweet pea. She folds her wings, opens them, and then flits to another flower to gather a more tasty bit of juice.

My ears open to the delicate hum of the whole bed, which makes the silence alive. And I concentrate upon the miracle of how a little protoplasm with tongue, nose, ears and eyes, feeds upon the hearts of the flowers. The world drops like a husk from the scales of my eyes. But before my brain-eye awakes, over and above the further eyes, the yellow butterfly with black dots upon her wings, has gone towards a large, dark lover, prancing like Martha Graham alongside her partner, and tracing an intricate confusion upon the limitless lens of my forehead.

I would fold them both within my brain-eye and understand the magic of their connection. I would become Euclid and, like him reconstruct the whole sensitive life of these butterflies through triangles. But all I can see is the path as they chase each other.

As I follow their movements idly, the texture of the evening presses upon my eyelids, and the pair vanishes.

And then there rises a slight breeze, shaking the sweet peas gently. And I see a suspensory group of stalkless blossoms no other than the butterflies in mass flight.

Eagerly, I search for the yellow one with black spots upon her wings. The last rays of the sun make the mist like the fiery wisps of smile rising from a volcanic crater.

And, above the luminous pendants, I can see the yellow

one, with dark spots, whom I would like to catch, flitting across the sun-warmed expanse.

Like Sindbad the sailor, waiting to go across the seas, I press my senses to the silence of expectation. The thickness of my fingers and the hardness of my body shame the nerve-ends and put me on edge. I cannot ever believe that a crude body may have, as an underlayer, a poet's lean soul.

I evolve a strategy. My cupped fingers will enclose the yellow one with dark spots within my grasp without hurting its wings or damaging its colours. And then I will look at beauty and release it.

These and a countless tremors of my senses urge me on. Multiplying the repertory of her movements, up, down, athwart, a liquid flow, curl, eddy, flitting with nimble wings, seeking contact with the hearts of many petals, she eludes my grasp.

The emptiness pours like sand through my fingers. And yet I am lured on to the chase by a primitive instinct, charged with vibrant feeling, drunk on the odour of sweet peas. In the aimlessness of my gaze, I feel an utter fulfillment.

Swift lie the meteor which she had seemed at first sight, uplifted by the breeze a little, with quivering wings, she darts out of my hands before they have closed upon her.

The hurt of the frustrated love possesses me. I revert back to the state of the amoeba in me and seek consolation beyond the primeval senses. But the capacity for thought has already been subtracted by anger from my self-perfection. And now I feel I can write a poem, for the experience of a lost love can thrive best on regrets and anger.

They, say, that, after the brief moments of rest, where they sip honey in the hearts of flowers, the butterflies go from luxuriant gardens to die in barren fields...

THE GOLDEN COCKEREL

The sun comes out over a pale blue sky and warms the earth, scattering the winter mist.

The golden cockerel has already announced the dawn from his perch on the manure pit, where he has been looking for worms. There is a certain agitation in his voice as he cukrooncroos.

Above the frail clatter of brass pots and pans, rubbed against the soft ashes the old woman shouts.

'Acha, acha, your mother-in-law is up and doing the chores!... Only your lazy wife has not opened her eyes...'

The cockerel cukrooncroos again.

'Yay, she is resting, after laying the eggs! Go and eat the ashes elsewhere! Shaitan!'

Stretching his neck to the full height of his elastic head, lifting the red crest, the cockerel sniffs at the fertilising warmth of the sun. Then he cuckrooncroos, as though the heat is coursing down his body. And he repeats his call, standing with unsculptured limbs on top of the little hillock.

'Go eat your masters or I will twist your ears!' the old woman quakes. And then she coughs a wheezy, asthmatic cough before talking to herself. 'Count them I must count the eggs before the children find them. They will break them.

And their father needs the strength...'

Far away, from above her, the sun bronzes her old face and makes it glisten. She feels the sap of youth in her body, as when she first came to this hut as a bride. She lifts the folds of her dupatta and hears it rustle against her breasts. But she lifts her gaze and sees the little chicks pecking at bits near the manure pit and capering behind their mother, the third hen.

The cockerel, who had been calling the faithful to prayer, has frozen into a statue. Then suddenly he leaps from the hillock and chases the third hen.

The hen shrieks and runs in an irregular movement, with uplifted feathers, head pushed forward and all her outer senses forbidding the approach of the suitor.

The cock breaks the fragile half steps of her panicky flight and grabs her neck. He makes for the doorway of the original female, the root from which heaven and earth spring.

With a shattering discordance of shrieks, she wards off his hold and spreads the confusion of her nerves into his body. His wings open and his feathers flutter, as though she is a cat attacking him in the dead haze of noon. And, for a moment, his eyes close, and he feels like a defeated murderer, full of avarice and anger.

The third hen has made good her escape.

The chicks follow her, startled but faithful to the mother, while she now stands as though to fold them under the shadow of her wings.

The sunlight steals over the soft grey dust of the early winter morning.

The cockerel rescues his equipoise and, as though he is the victor of the love fray, flashes up, with bright feathers outspread, on to the manure pit, and cuckrooncroos again.

The old woman stoops to gather the pots and pans and, clearing her throat again, says:

'To be sure, you inhabit the throat of a God! Talky talk! Cocky Cock! Shame upon you! Your third wife ran away!'

Quivering in his entrails, at the compliments and insults, the cockerel sniffs the air like a peacock, lifts his neck agilely, stands on one foot, on the rubbish heap, cuckrooncrooing away as though to show off the purple cone of his crest against the sunlight...

THE PEACOCK

After the long wait of many gasping hours the rains have come. The eyes are filled with seven shades of green. And the children have put upon the swings.

Deep from within the fields, come the cries of the peacock calling to the peahens.

And there, beyond the grove over the well, a pair alights, But, contrary to the expectations aroused by the song of the male calling the female, it is the peahen who is hot on the trail of the peacock.

Turning to look and make sure that he is seen, gracefully lifting one foot forward and then the other, the male bird walks masterfully ahead.

Afraid that she may lose him if he flies off again, the

female bird treads the earth meditatively like the Nayika, vigilant, with longing in her eyes.

And now, holding the female in his spell, speechless but sure of step, the peacock is bound up in a prolonged repose, sniffing at the air, and pecking at the odd bits of grain, and considering the female, as part of the landscape. Then, he senses the nearness of the female. And then arises in him a wave of desire, as in the heart of a prolific pigeon.

He turns again to look at his spouse, as though to lure her on in pursuit. And he sees that look in her eyes which seems to say: 'I have sought you all day in vain.'

Seeing the obvious devotion in her worshipful stare, the proud male bird turns away from the adorer.

The peahen wilts and nearly gives up the chase.

Pondering for a moment on how he may tantalise the female, again, the peacock rushes forward suddenly, then rests till the peahen has reached him, but again sidetracks her, waiting to be caught. And for a while the pair repeat these movements, as though they are playing hide and seek in a maze.

'I have found you,' she shrieks in the loveplay, as she nearly comes up to him.

'I don't want you,' he says.

And then mustering all the power in the sinews of his flesh, he struts, prances, shifting to this side and that, drunkenly describes a circle, and, revolving his head, begins to stamp on his feet and dance.

The ripeness of the senses is in the change of his heart.

Shaping his passion in measured tresses, he compels a rhythm in his steps which seems to overtake his desire. Drawing near her, withdrawing, he lures her on, with her day-worn heart aflame.

And, stirring his plumage, as though he is aware of his power, he now faces' her, full face, pecking at her beak, only to murder her hopes by stepping aside.

At last the very sight of the stretch of his refulgent body holds her content.

And once feared, then adored and longed for, he unfolds for her the vision of his body, in the uplifted outspread tail.

Is it a ray of humility that turns his eyes now to his ugly feet? Or is it the self-torment, as they say in our village, in appeasement of his colossal male vanity?

A LEAF IN THE STORM

Once upon a time, there was a leaf, on the branch of a tree, a little leaf, tender like a parrot's bosom.

There were other leaves on the tree. Small lovely leaves. And big leaves which were paling with age and ready to drop off, on the brink of death.

But the little leaf that was tender like the parrot's bosom, was neither too small nor too big-it was young like the dawn. The lines on its palm were forming as though its fate was being set.

One day there came a breeze, which was not the breeze of Punjab. No one knew where it came from. Perhaps it came form the sky like a windstorm. It shook the whole tree. And it left the little leaf, which was tender like the parrot's bosom, torn, so that the lines on its palm-like body began to change, And, suddenly, it began to sway, and sing a song, which was not the song of the land of the five rivers.

Every day, the same breeze blew, sharper than the first windstorm.

And one day, it uprooted the tree. And, catching the little leaf, which was tender like the parrot's bosom, in its mouth, the breeze blew away...

Swaying gently, sad and alone, the leaf fell on an earth, where the sun did not shine, and where there was no warmth like that in the land of the five rivers. A pallor came over it, not with age, but the yellowing which the moist air produces, where there is no sunshine.

Long did the leaf languish in exile, thinking that just as the leaf from the Bodhi tree had taken root in Lanka, so it had flown across the seas, But it did not know that the leaf which had flown to Lanka had a root attached to it, while its own roots lay drying in the land of the five rivers.

At last, aflame with ambition, it prepared to fly like a bird, and it took off from its foreign habitation.

Swaying gently, frolicking, playing, singing a song, it flew and flew and flew...

And it came and settled on a rock, like a bird returning to its own landscape, after the seasonal flight.

The sun rays warmed its heart. The rains came and quenched its thirst. And it drifted for sustenance on to some roots, which were jutting out of the crevices of mountains.

If you see it now, the lines on its palm are formed, as though its destiny was always clear.

And it sits there like a premature Buddha, baking itself in the fire of the sun, to resemble the colour of its own.

They say that there are magic trees which spread their roots from the sky downwards on to the soil. The uprooted leaf seems to feel that even the drifting leaf might, one day, become a tree with real roots, but with leaf roots such as itself can uproot themselves at will and fly away to another soil for a while. For it is necessary to have roots but not to get rooted in barren fields...

6

Little Chicks*

Pecking, pecking, pecking... Pecking here, pecking there, pecking nowhere in particular. The three little chicks toddle up before the kitchen doorstep, where I have thrown the remainders of the lentils for the sparrows.

Slightly agitated, jumping a step or two, darting away from near the mother hen, but running back for shelter at the sight of the slightest shadow, Brownie, Blackie and Ginger are like tied balls of cotton, except for their perkey little yellow beaks.

I scatter the remainders of the dish of rice into the flower bed.

Up toddles Brownie, the most forward one.

Blackie follows suit, perhaps being the second big one in age.

Ginger is left behind, but makes up for his littleness by outflanking others, straying aimlessly on the side and then clambering up towards the grain.

---

* From *Between Tears and Laughter.*

Browine and Blackie peck a trifle more furiously and edge Ginger away.

Whereupon, the mother hen instinctively goes to the rescue of her littlest one, not dramatically, but by a kind of casual moment of her neck uplifted, as though to warn others of her displeasure.

Moti, the mongrel dog, starved for days, has been dolefully eyeing the chicks and admiring their courage in getting so near the shadow of my presence.

I feel I ought to throw him a bone, but desist because this will frighten the hen, or the chicks, and then I shall not be able to see how the little specks of life struggle for survival.

For a moment, I watch the miracle of littleness trying to go forward.

Pecking, pecking, pecking, the life of the chicks would seem to be concentrated in their beaks. And the globules of their soft woolen rotundities seem to be borne along by the intensity of their hunger. Is it possible that more than half of the nonchalance of the hen, who is not interfering with her chicks and is allowing them to have their fill, while she looks soulfully on, is to guard them against the danger of a 'shoo' from me.

And how can Moti sit there patiently, without daring to come near me, because, perhaps, he has been given moral lessons in good behaviour, with 'Dure! Dure!' and an occasional lifting of the fuel stick by the Mali's wife who guards her dishes against pollution almost like a Brahmin lady.

Pecking, pecking, pecking, asserting their right to live, the little chicks have now dared to climb up the steps leading to the kitchen, an inch or two from where I stand.

I stiffen myself into the rectitude of non-hurting and try to radiate complete ahimsa.

But the hen advances towards her brood, cluck-clucking a little and warns the little ones against me.

I withdraw.

The mere shadow of movement has frightend Brownie, Blackie and Ginger. And, perkily, they jump aside, doing their first exercise in vigilance against the best called man. Their panic brings the mother hen cluck-clucking to their aid.

The woman of the house thinks I have deliberately frightened the chicks and scolds me.

I am shame-filled. But I am not really feeling guilty.

Moti comes slinking by, mops up the remainders of the lentils, sniffs around for more and then looks to me.

I throw the bone for him.

Browine, Blackie and Ginger come pecking back to the grain, as soon as the ominous shadow of me is removed from within the orbit of their mother's eyes.

The miracle goes on.

Part II

TEARS AT THE HEART OF THINGS

7

Lajwanti*

The loo of May flew into Lajwanti's face like flames from the hearth of heaven. The sun from whose mouth the fiery breeze came seemed to be standing relentlessly behind, her, even as her heavy jowled brother-in-law, Jaswant, often stood, apparently to goad her on to work but really to draw her attention to himself. And, as the sweat moistened her hands, she tightened her grip on the handle of the cage in which her Maina bird sat, docile and dumb, under the oppression of the heat. But she persisted in her determination to trudge along to Gurgaon, where she hoped to catch the bus to her father's house in Pataudi.

'Talk to me Maina-say something!

The Maina bird fluttered in the cage, perhaps to indicate to Lajwanti that she was alive.

'I will give you water as soon as I get to the bus stop'.

And, urged by the heat spots on her feet where the torn soles of her chappals exposed her flesh, she hurried towards the shade of a solitary mango tree which stood a little way

---

* From *Lajwanti and Other Stories.*

away from the Mehrauli-Gurgaon road.

Once in the cool, she phewed several hot breaths, wiped the nape of her neck with the end of her head cloth, then forgetfully smudged her face with the soiled dupatta, licked her palate with her tongue, put down the cage of the Maina bird, and looked in the direction of Gurgaon.

The dense heatmist enveloped everything. But, beyond the green grove of mangoes, half a mile ahead, she could see the outline of the old caravanserai.

Quickly, she lifted the cage and went forward. She had the echo augury that Jaswant would be hot on her trail, as soon as her mother-in-law realised that she, Lajwanti, had not returned from the well for more than two hours. And he had a bicycle.

'Come then my little Maina, we shall soon be there...'

The exalted bungalows of the police lines of Gurgaon, sequestered behind hedges, under tall trees, quenched the thirst of her eyes. The green leaves of neem trees were like cool sherbet to her spirit. And there seemed to be a confectioner's shop where she might be able to drink a tumbler of whey and give the Maina a little feed and water.

Somehow, the last lap of a foot journey is always the most arduous. Her legs seemed to drag along. And the burning on the exposed parts of her soles became unbearable. And the echo augury about Jaswant catching up on her enveloped her mind. And she was nearly at the end of her tether. And yet she pushed forward, as though she was possessed by the demon of flight.

There was a moment of weakening as the Maina became utterly still; and, without looking to see, she felt that the bird might have fainted with the heat and died.

And in the panic of this premonition, she felt the chords of guilt choke her dry throat: She might have borne the humiliation. She might have given in to Jaswant. She could have closed her eyes. Her husband Balwant was away at College. Her benevolent father-in-law would not have known. And the mother-in-law, who wanted son's son, more than anything else, would not have worried, even if she had come to know, because she favoured Jaswant, who worked on the land and not Balwant who wanted to be a clerk.

'Talk to me Maina... Don't go away from me... If you go I too will be finished...'

As the bird did not even flutter, her heart seemed to sink, and the sweat just poured down her body.

'Maybe, I am being superstitious,' she said to herself. 'I should have done a magic ceremony on the cross-roads of Hauz Khas to ensure my safe arrival in Pataudi. And, then God would have kept my enemies dispersed...'

Destiny spread the length of dumb distance before her, however. And, facing the emptiness, she felt as though the whole earth was opposed to her. And she wanted to kneel down before the Almighty for all the sins for which she was being punished.

'Oh gently, gently, show me the path!' she cried out in her soul.

At that juncture, she heard the sinister shout of Jaswant:

'Stop, mad woman, or I shall kill you!'

She did not look back, because she knew the authentic accent of her brother-in-law's voice. She merely ran, with the instinct to fly, to get away, out of his reach, to the group of men who were resting by the confectioner's shop.

The Maina bird fluttered its wings wildly. And now that it apprehended disaster, it shrieked and cried.

'Stop...' The voice of doom repeated itself.

Descending into the pit of confusion. Lajwanti was lost in the primal jungle of turmoil. The tortures of hell awaited her. But, perhaps she could make it.

"Lajwanti," Jaswant called in a more mellow voice.

This startled her, weakened her, and made her regret she had not given in.

She fairly ran, about twenty yards before the confectioner's shop. Jaswant passed by her, on his bicycle. Then he descended and, putting the machine athwart, barred her way.

Lajwanti conjured up in her downcast eyes the smile of horror that beamed on his heavy, pockmarked face.

She swerved away and outflanked him by diving into the ditch and making for the confectioner's shop from the side of the depression.

He dragged the bicycle and raced up to her.

After he had reached the confectioner's shop, he dropped the machine and ran towards her with an enveloping movement.

Lajwanti fell into his outstretched arms almost like a willing victim.

But once she became aware of the hard embrace of the wild beast, she recoiled back, to free herself.

Again she ran.

Startled, he turned and chased her, catching, her by the headcloth before she could sit down on the wooden bench by the confectioner's shop.

'Why did you run away?' he asked. 'Have you no shame?... Look, folks...'

The straggling peasants looked nonchalantly at the scene, without coming any nearer. And three school boys came and stared.

'Let me go — I want to go to my father's house,' Lajwanti said, without lifting her gaze to Jaswant.

The Maina bird fluttered in the cage.

'No, you are returning to your husband's home!' Jaswant ground the words. And he twisted her wrist as she tried to get out of his grasp.

'Brute!' she cried. And, without shedding any tears, she began to sob. 'Leave me alone!... Let me give the Maina some water to drink...'

The throttling growth of Jaswant's bestiality gripped her young body and he shouted hoarsely:

'Prostitute! Bad woman! Running away!...

What will our brotherhood think? — you disgracing us like this!...'

Lajwanti collapsed in a huddle at his feet.

The brother-in-law hit her with his right foot.

At this the confectioner half got up from his greasy cushion and appealed:

'Ohe, do not hit her. Persuade her to go back with you...' But as the woman sat mutely like a bundle, the tangled undergrowth of Jaswant's emotions became concentrated into the fury of his stubborn, frustrated will. He slapped her on the head with his loose right hand.

Lajwanti gave herself to the torment and sat dumbly, suppressing even her sobs.

And now a crowd of passers-by gathered to see the fun, but no one intervened.

The grip of frightfulness lingered in the crevices of light before Lajwanti's hooded eyes.

Grating of brakes and the dragging of wheels brought Engineer Din Dayal's jeep to a sudden halt, twenty yards ahead of the confectioner's shop.

'Go quickly', Shrimati Sushila Dayal ordered her husband. 'I saw him slapping the woman.'

'Let us find out what's what before getting excited,' said the dour, taciturn engineer. And he turned to the confectioner: 'What has happened? Who are they?'

'Sir, it seems the girl has run away from her father-in-law's house and wants to go to her father's house... But her brother-in-law came and caught her...'

Shrimati Dayal jumped out of the jeep and ran ahead of her husband.

'Cowards! Get aside! Looking on! As though this is a fun fair!'

The crowd scattered and revealed Jaswant holding Lajwanti by the head cloth, which he had twisted into his hand with the plait of her hair.

'Leave her alone!' Shrimati Dayal ordered.

'Sister, she has ran away from her husband's house,' appealed Jaswant. 'And our good name is at stake!'

'She must have come away for a good reason,' Shrimati Dayal said.

'Where has she come from?'

'From near Hauz Khas,' Jaswant said.

'Hai-on foot?.. Ten miles? She has walked.'

Jaswant nodded his head.

'Poor child!' Shrimati Dayal said turning to her husband.

'I will not allow the girl to die of a heat stroke. Put her in the jeep and let us take her home.'

'I will not let her go now that I have caught her' Jaswant said timid but frontal.

'I will call the police and hand you over!' threatened Shrimati Dayal.

'Anyhow,' Engineer Din Dayal counselled Jaswant, 'Come and talk things over at my house... Persuade her to go back with you. Don't force her...'

'Come along,' said Shrimati Dayal lifting Lajwanti even as she brusquely extricated the twisted plait of the girl's hair our of Jaswant's grip.

'Give me the Maina to hold,' Jaswant bullied his sister-in-law.

Lajwanti merely nodded her head in negation and proceeded.

In the cool shade of the verandah of Engineer Dayal's bungalow, Lajwanti removed the hood of her headcloth and revealed her tender, tear-striken eyes and said:

'Give me some water for the Maina, mother.' 'Gurkha,' Shrimati Dayal called her servant. 'Give some cool water to all of us... make it lime and water... Simple water for the bird...'

The servile Gurkha, more taciturn than the engineer, took in everything at a glance and went towards the kitchen.

'Why did you beat the girl? Shrimati Dayal asked Jaswant.

'Time after time we have told her,' said Jaswant, 'That her husband has only one year more to do at college before he finishes his B.A. But she wishes to be with him or go to her father's house.'

'Mother, he is a liar!' Lajwanti shrieked.

'You must have oppressed her very much to make her say

this of you!' said engineering Dayal.

'Sire, we have been good to her,' pleaded Jaswant. 'She comes from a poor home. My father is Chaudhuri Ganga Ram, Sarpanch of the whole village... I have a wife too, but she is a gentle woman from a big house...'

'Like a cow,' Lajwanti flared up. 'And you want many more views.'

'Don't bark!' — Shameless one! Or I will hit you!'

Jaswant said.

At this Shrimati Dayal got up with a cool deliberation of her torso and delivered a clean slap on Jaswant's face and said:

'How do you like this? — If someone else hits you'!'.

The man was taken completely unawares. He sat with his mouth open but speechless.

'That is what I should have done when he tried to approach me!' said Lajwanti, her head turned demurely away from the engineer.

'Clearly, this girl is not happy with your family.' said the Engineer. 'Let her go back to her father's house till her husband has finished his studies. And then she can come back to your family.'

'That is right!' added Shrimati Dayal. 'I will not allow the child to be in your grip. You can have one wife and not two...'

In the quivering scale pans of balance, created by the voices of injustice, Lajwanti felt the first moment of calm which had come to her during two long years. But immediately she felt the fear of Jaswant's revenge for the slap he had received on the face. She looked at the Maina and said in speechless speech: 'Angel, suppose there is a cool place, somewhere in the world where we two can rest..'

'Ask her to decide,' Jaswant said, 'If she goes to her father's house, she can never come back to us. If she comes back with me, we might consider sending her for a little while to her father's house.'

'Tell him what you feel, girl?' said Shrimati Dayal.

'I want to go to my father's house, and never want to set foot on their threshold again,' answered Lajwanti.

'There!' said Shrimati Dayal. 'That is her answer for you... and if you are a decent man, go back to your home. I will see the girl to the bus which takes her to Pataudi...' And, she turned to her husband for confirmation of her decision.

'That's right!' the Engineer said. 'Gurkha!' Shrimati Dayal called.

'Coming, Bibiji, the servant answered. And he appeared with lime water for all and a little plain water and cummin seed for the Maina bird.

Lajwanti arrived with the cage of the Maina bird in her hand, at her father's house, when the old man was just going out to bathe his buffalo at the well. He stood open-eyed and open-mouthed, asking himself whether what he saw was his daughter or her ghost. When she bent down to take the dust off his feet, he could smell the acrid summer sweat of her clothes and knew that it was Lajwanti. He dared not look at her face, because a daughter coming back home without due ceremony, was inauspicious. Gentle as he was, however, he did not ask any questions. Only, he called to his young son, who was chopping up fodder for the buffalo.

'Indu, your eldest sister has come. Wake up, your little sister, Moti...'

Lajwanti was sad for her father. She knew that a man who had borne the grinding pressures of years of survival on one bigha and a buffalo, and whose wife had died leaving him with two small children, was in no condition to receive a grown-up married daughter, who had returned without even the proverbial bundle of clothes to change into.

Indu left into the chopper and rushed towards her, clinging to her legs as though he saw the ghost of his mother standing by the door. To be sure, Lajwanti looked the split image of her mother. Only mother had become sallow with lungs, while Lajo's colouring was pucca brown, and gave richness to the small even face, with the fine nose, flawed by a big tatoo mark on her chin.

Tears welled into Lajwanti's eyes at the warmth of the boy's embrace.

'Look at this poor Maina,' she said. 'She had come all the way with me from New Delhi.'

The young boy grabbed the cage from his sister's hand and soon forgot about Lajwanti in the effort to make the bird talk.

'I should give her some lentils to eat and a little water,' Lajwanti said, sitting on the threshold of the verandah.

'Then she might talk to you... Though, I hope she does not say too much... The neighbours will know everything...'

For now that she was here, she wanted her return, somehow, to remain a private occurrence. She knew, of course, that everyone in a small place knew everyone else's business. And she had no hope of escaping censure from the tongues which had wagged when, before her marriage, she had played openly with boys of her own age, and seldom cared to cover her head with her dupatta because she did not want to look like a ghost. All the elders called her 'Man Lajo,' while the boys called her, 'Meena Kumari' after the film heroine she resembled. She wanted as she sat there, to know what was in her father's heart — whether he had understood her mysterious will, and the instinct which had inspired her always to do the odd things. He had always told her that he was sorry he had named her Lajwanti, which means sensitive plant, because she has lived up to her name. Indu pushed a cup of water into her bird's cage. And lo! the Maina began to talk.

'Lajo, what does she say?' the boy asked.

Lajwanti smiled, even as she looked at the torrid sky.

After her father returned from the well, he tied the buffalo and put what cattle food Indu had chopped up before the animal. As the boy had not cut enough, he took the chopper and began to prepare more. He was not the kind to scold anyone, and least of all did he want to blame his son for getting excited about his elder sister.

When the buffalo had been looked after, he proceeded to

soak the lentils for the evening meals and proceeded to light the fire.

'I will do all that, Bapu: Lajwanti said.

'Daughter, it does not matter,' he answered and stubbornly went on with the chores. And, turning to his son, he said,' 'give your sister a mat to sit on.'

Imperceptible as were his feelings behind the mask of his calm, wrinkled face, she saw a pallor on his lips as he said this, and she knew that she was not wanted. That mat was only given to guests.

The courtyard was filled with shadows long before the fire in the sky became ashes. Lajwanti could see the clouds tinted red as though the world had witnessed some gruesome murder.

And, frightened of her own self, she tried to hold her breath.

'Sister, I have brought you a pitcher of water to bathe with, 'Indu said.

Before Lajwanti could answer, Moti had been disturbed by her brother's voice and awakened, whining.

Lajwanti leaped forward to her and embraced the child, consoling her.

'Lajo,' her father said, 'The children want a mother. And I would have kept you here and not given you away, if people had not begun to talk about you...' He paused after this statement for a long time, and then after blowing at the hearth fire, he continued: Now, I am both father and mother to them... and, as for you, I will take you back to your parents-in-law's house. I shall fall at their feet and ask them to forgive you. The disgrace of your widowhood without your becoming a widow is unbearable... They will only call you ugly names here... They do not know that you are 'sensitive plant'...

Two days later, a post card came addressed to Shri Hari Ram, father of Lajwanti, written by Jaswant, on behalf of his father, saying, that as Lajwanti had run away, without permission from her husband or her parents-in-law, the clothes she had brought on her wedding were being returned and that no one in Delhi was now willing to see her 'black face'.

Old Hari had already been trying to arrange for someone to look after his buffalo, his son and his daughter, so that he could take Lajwanti back to her parents-in-law. He had sent for the midwife, who had delivered all these children, from Pataudi proper, because he did not know anyone in the small village, who would oblige, without the payment of some cash.

Fortunately, the midwife Champa, arrived on the same morning after the post card was received. And she was more than willing, to take on the job of looking after the household.

'Why,' she said, 'I had hoped to see our Lajo with belly. And I had waited to be called to her bedside, so that I could deliver her of a son. And, now, my loved one, you are here, without a sign in your eyes of the coming of the happy event. If only for the sake of the soul of your dear mother, go, hurry back. And come soon with your lap full of a child...'

'I am putting my turban at your feet,' said old Hari Ram to Chaudhri Ganga Ram, literally removing his enormous crown of cloth from his head and placing it on the shoes of his daughter's father-in-law.

"Oh, come and sit here with me;" answered Chaudhri Ganga Ram, brushing the beadstead with his left hand as he smoked the hookah under the shade of a neem tree.

Lajwanti crouched a little way away, with her face covered by her head cloth and averted her gaze from her father-in-law towards the torrid fields; Her heart was in her mouth, lest her brother-in-law, Jaswant, might suddenly appear form the barn, or even her mother-in-law, come on the scene suddenly before the father-in-law had forgiven her. At the same time, she knew that there would be no forgiveness, but only a reluctant nod to indicate that she could stay.

The nod of approval was, however, long in coming. For Chaudhri Ganga Ram kept silent, after having lifted Hari Ram to sit by him, and only his hookah spoke a little agitatedly.

Meanwhile, Lajwanti felt the sweat gathering on the nape of her head and flowing down her spine. And she looked at her blessed Maina in the cage to see if the bird was not dead. The journey had been easier this time, because they had come by bus from Pataudi to Gurgaon and then caught the connection from Gurgaon to the bus stop half a mile away from the little village of her father-in-law. And as the bird seemed still, she spoke to her in wordless words:

'My Maina tell me what will happen now? My heart flutters, as you often do when you are frightened of the cat coming to eat you. And I do not know if Jaswant will relent and not pursue me any more. But perhaps now that my father has brought me back, I will allow myself to be eaten. Only the humiliation will be complete now. Oh if only I had warmed to him and not thought of my own man who would never have known! I am really defeated. And even words are no use... And yet within me there is desire, and there is life — a river of feelings like the ancient Saraswati river which has gone underground and disappeared from the surface... How shall I control those feelings, those prisoners, trying to burst out...'

She opened her eyes to make sure. The vision was real.

Involuntarily, her eyes closed and a sigh got muffled into the folds of her headcloth. Sparks like stars shot out of the darkness of her head, and the agitation of nerves pushed up a copious sweat all over her. She knew that the constellations in the sky above her were ominous.

'So the dead one has turned up!' the mother-in-law's voice came, as the old woman returned from the well with one. pitcher on her head and another one on her left arm. The heavy breathing of the woman, forced to fetch and carry and do all the chores in the absence of Lajwanti, accented her voice with bitterness.

'She is your daughter,' said old Hari Ram to appease the woman. In his innocence he imagined that the proverbial mother-in-law had become the cause of his daughter's flight. 'I have brought her back... the midwife, Champa, said that the girl has made a mistake...'

'To be sure,' answered the mother-in-law. 'There was no question, since Balwant has not been back from Kalej for more than a few days at a time...

Unless she has cast the spell of her grey eyes on someone else... Jaswant says he has seen her winking at the visitors on the roadside...'

'We are respectable people,' said Chaudhri Ganga Ram to reinforce his wife's speech.

'I... what shall I say, Chaudhriji,' answered Hari Ram meekly. 'I wish fate had made her not so good looking... But,' now, I have brought her back. And you can kill her if she looks at another... Here is a ring for my son Balwant. I could not give much dowry. Now I will make up a little for what the boy did not get...'

From the wearisome acceptance of her fate, there swirled up incomprehensible violent urges of truth in Lajwanti, so that she shook a little and was on the point of telling them the horrible facts. And she was mad at her father for effacing himself and bowing before her in-laws. But the tremors in her entrails ended in choking her throat. And the lofty flights of anger only befogged her brain.

'Jaswant! Jaswant!... Come over here...' the mother-in- law called her eldest son.

The scarecrow in the field turned round. Then he lifted the palm of his hand to see. He understood. And he began to walk back.

In the silence of doom, Lajwanti quivered as though the demons of hell had let loose snakes and scorpions on her body. And, in a fit of crazy abandon, she felt herself borne form the underworld, on a bed, by her heroic husband, his arms wrapped around her... Actually, beneath the trembling flesh, she knew Balwant to be a coward, who dare not even raise his head to look at his elder brother.

'She has come back!' Jaswant ground the words in his mouth, throwing the white radishes away on the ground near the outdoor kitchen.

'She could not tell you that she wanted to see the midwife,' old Hari Ram said. 'It was a false alarm.'

'There are mid-wives here also!' Jaswant answered pat. 'Why there is the Safdarjung Hospital!...' Do no be taken in by her stories, Uncle. She has looked at more than one before her marriage... She is just a bad girl!... The way she insulted me when I went to fetch her back,... She sat, there, answering back! And allowed that Afsar's wife to slap me on the face!... Prostitute!...'

'Bus! bus! Son!' Chaudhri Ganga Ram said to restrain the boy.

'Take that for having me beaten!' Jaswant said and kicked Lajwanti on her behind, 'Lajwanti quivered, then veered round, almost doubled over, and uttered a shrill cry before beginning to sob.

'You deserved a shoe beating!' shouted Jaswant, towering over the girl like an eagle in a malevolent glee of power, his arms outstretched as though he was going to hit her again.

'Come away!' shouted his father.

'Let him punish her if he thinks she has done wrong,' said Hari Ram. And let her fall at his feet... My daughter is pure... After saying this he felt pangs of remorse at his own cowardice and he was caught in the paroxysm of a dry throated cough, and water filled his eyes.

'Maina, my maina,' Lajwanti said under her breath, 'I cannot bear this...'

'Deceitful cunning wretch!' Jaswant said and he turned away towards her father. 'Take her away... We have no use for her here! After she has disgraced us before the whole brotherhood'

'Not so many angry words, son!' Chaudhri Ganga Ram said. 'You have punished her enough!'

'Son, let her get up and work!' mother-in-law said.

'Bless your words of wisdom' said Hari Ram. 'I knew you would be merciful... And now I leave her in your care. Kill her if you like. But don't let her come to me without her lap full of son. I shall not be able to survive the disgrace if she comes again...'

'Maina, my maina, who will talk to you, if I go away forever?' Lajwanti asked the bird in the cage even as she washed her with palmfuls of water from the bucket.

The bird fluttered wildly evading the shower.

'Will you shriek if I drown you in the water, my little one?' Lajwanti asked.

The bird edged away as though in answer.

And she sat down on the ledge of the well, away from the surging waters which were all around her dizzy brain.

If she stopped to think, she felt she would never do it... It was now or never, when there was no one on the well except herself and the Maina. The village women had finished fetching the water for the evening. And soon it would be dark.

From where she sat, a tilt — that would do it.

But no, She must not wait any more.

And with a jerk of her torso, interrupted by her indecision, she forced herself into a heave.

The fall was ugly. Her left shoulder hit the stone on the side before she fell sideways into the well.

For a moment, she was limp.

The impact of the fall took her full-length into the water.

But, in a second, she felt her body rising up as though. from its own momentum. Unfortunately, for her she was a swimmer. She could not decide to let go of her breath. And, now, her hand pushed up above the water. And she found herself using her arms, to keep afloat.

Still there was a chance.

Rising from the torso, she ducked down, with her nose tweaked between her fingers.

She stayed under the water for a minute and then tried to drown herself by letting go of her hand from the tweaked nose.

The head rose above the water, panting for breath.

'Lajwanti! Lajwanti! Bad one come out! her mother-in-law's voice came, in a shrill appeal. 'This is not the way of respectable people...'

There was no way by which Lajwanti could put her head into the water. Perhaps she really did not want to die. How had the old woman turned up? Because, left to herself, she would have gone under with a second or third try. Not even in the darkness, was there an escape... Above the well, life would be worse hell than even before...

Gently, she let go. And then water began to fill her nostrils and her mouth. And she was submerged.

Before she had lost consciousness, however, she felt herself lying down in the slush near the well.

They were pressing her belly. Some one was sitting on her. And the spurts of water oozed from her nostrils and mouth. The rancid tastes of stale air was on her palate-the taste of life's breath.

And as she lay dissolving under her heavy eyelids, the bitterness of her breath seemed to lapse, and sleep shaped her eyes into a fixed stare.

And yet, within a moment, more water had come up through her nose and mouth.

And, within her, she could hear her foolish, tormented heart pounding away.

And then the drowsy eyelids opened. And she could see the Maina bird in the cage by her.

'Alas' She said in wordless words, above the ache of the head and the thumping of the heart, 'There is no way for me... I am... condemned to live...'

8

The Parrot in the Cage*

'Rukmaniai, ni Rukmaniai' the parrot in the cage called in the way Rukmani's friends used to call her when they entered the alley way of Kucha Chabuk Swaran in Lahore. And he repeated the call even before she could answer his as she used to do when she wanted to humour the bird. She did not answer but sat crouching on the fringe of the road about half a furlong away from the Amritsar court.

'Rukmaniai, ni Rukmaniai! the parrot called again.

She was peering though the little clouds of dust raised by the passing motors and tongas and yekkas in the direction from which, she had been told by the roasted gram stall-keeper, the *Dipty Collator* was to come and she remained heedless to the parrot's cry.

'Rukmaniai, ni Rukmaniai!' the parrot called shrilly and went on repeating the cry with the sure mocking bird's instinct that if he kept on calling her she would answer.

---

* From *Reflections on The Golden Bed and other Stories.*

'Han, my son, han... the old woman said after all, wearily. There had been a dull ache behind the small knot of hair on the back of her head and, now, with the mounting heat of the September morning, it seemed to her like the rumblings of the dreadful night when murder and fire had raged in her lane.

Little rivulets of sweat trickled through the deep fissures of old age which lined her face and she shaded her eyes, with the inverted palm of her hand, to probe the sunlight more surely for the vision of the Deputy Commissioner.

Her contracted, toothless mouth was open and only a couple of flies came from the direction in which she looked and settled on the corners of her lips.

She waved her left hand gingerly to scatter the flies. But they persisted and set up an irritation in her soul through which she felt a panic seize her belly.

'Ni tun kithe hain?' the parrot cried another cry which he had learnt from the old woman's friends who invariably asked on entering the lane, 'Where are you?' For she used to be away earning her living as a maid of all work, cleaning utensils for the people in the bigger houses in the lane or was mostly hidden from view in the inner sanctums of the dark ground floor room by the well in the gulley.

'Son, I don't know where I am...' she said listlessly, in the effort to keep the parrot quiet by assuring him she was taking notice of him, 'I only know that if Fate has not given me her burqah to escape with, I should not be here...'

'Ni tun ki karni hain?' the parrot persisted with the third call which Rukmani's friends used to call.

'Nothing, son, I am doing nothing... only waiting... the old woman said tiredly, as though now she was holding a metaphorical conversation with her pet to keep her mind occupied. For, from her entrails arose a confusion which was like the panic she had felt at the mad throats bursting with shouts of 'Allah ho Akbar!' 'Har har Mahadev!' 'Sat Sri Akal!' on the night of terror when she had fled from the lane.

There had been flashes of blazing light; cracking of burning housebeams; smoke, smoke, choking smoke... And she had thought that her last days had come, that the earth itself was troubled through the misdeeds of the *Kaliyug* and that soon the *dharti* would open up and swallow everything... And then Fato had come and told her she would be murdered if she did not leave.

'Ni tun ki karni hain?' the parrot repeated.' *Ni tun kithe hain*?...'

'Nothing son, nothing', Rukmani answered,' And I don't know where I am... And as she looked steadily towards the junction of the Mall Road and Kutchery Road and saw no sign of the Deputy Commissioner, her last phrase seemed to get meaning.

'Rukmaniai, ni Rukmaniai! the parrot called again. Her answers to his metallic, shrill, nasal cries did not irritate her anymore, but relieved the heavy pressure of the demons of the dreadful night on her head and her chest and her bowels.

'Ni tun ki karni hain?' the parrot persisted.

'Son, I am waiting for the Sahib, so that he can give me some money to buy bread with...' They say that the Congress Sarkar will give back what we have lost, son, they say — I heard at the *station,* son, at the *station?...* Are you hungry my son — you must be hungry I shall buy you some gram from that stall keeper when the Sahib gives me money... '

'Mai, you are dreaming! You have gone mad!' the gram stall keeper said. 'Go, go your way to the town, you may get some food at the Durbar Sahib temple. You won't get anything from the *Dipty Collator...*'

'*Vay, jaja,* eater of your masters! she shouted bitterly. Such commonsense as that of the complacent gram seller seemed to break the pitcher of her hopes. And she mooed like a cow in defiance at the end of her speech.

'Acha, don't abuse me. I only said this for your own good,' the stall keeper answered as he whisked the flies off his stall with the end of a dirty apron.

'On, why did I leave home to wander like this from door to door!' old Rukmani whined almost under her breath. 'Oh why did you have to turn me out of my room in my old age, God... Oh why... Why didn't I tie the rupees I had earned in a knot on my dupatta!... Hai Rabba!...

She moaned to herself, and tremors of tenderness went swirling through her flesh. And tears filled her eyes. And in the hazy dust before her the violent rhythms of the terrors of falling houses and dying, groaning men and heavy, shouting men, danced in macabre trembling waves of sunlight, dim and unsubstantial like the ghosts on a cremation ground before whom she had always cowered every time she had attended a funeral.

'Rukmaniai, ni Rukmaniai!' the parrot called and brought her to herself.

Crackling flames of heat now assailed her. And she sweated more profusely. And yet she crouched where she was only shuffling like a hen sitting over her eggs.

'At least go and sit under the shade of the tree,' the gram seller said.

The pupils of her eyes were blistering with the glare. She wiped her face with the end of her dupatta and heaved as though she was lifting the weight of a century's miseries up with her. Then she took the handle of the iron cage in which her pet parrot sat and bent-backed but staring ahead, ambled up to a spot where the precarious shadow of a kikar tree lay on the rutted earth.

Ni tun ki kithe hain? ni...' the parrot's monologue continued. So did her self-communings, aroused by the anonymous, meaningless repetitive calls; 'Nowhere, son, nothing, nothing...'

She had hardly settled down when suddenly a motor whirred past, with a motor cyclist ahead and some policemen in a jeep behind, scattering much dust on the fringe of the roadside.

'There goes your *"Dipty Collator"* said the gram stall keeper.

'Hai hai!' Come my son! she screamed as she shot up with great alacrity and picked up the cage in her hand. 'Come I will join my hands to the Sahib and fall at this feet. "Mad woman!' the gram seller said cynically.

She heeded him not, but penetrated the clouds of dust.

Behind her, and on all sides, she could hear the sound of rushing feet storming towards the gloomy gates of the kutchery. And their cries whirled in the air. 'Hujoor, Mai Bap, hear us' 'Sarkar!' *"Dipty Saheb"*... We have come on foot all the way from Lahore... You...' She nearly fell as the more powerful men among the crowed brushed past her and their own women.

'Rukmaniai! *Tun kithe hain?'* the parrot in the cage cried even as he fluttered his wings in a panic at the voices and the hurtling feet.

The old woman did not answer but sped grimly on. Only, in a moment, the dust storm which was proceeding towards the court was turned back by a furious whirlwind from the opposite direction. A posse of policemen charged the refugees with lathis and angry shouts which drowned the chorus of voices of which Rukamani's sighs and her parrot's cries had been a part.

In the delirium of motion which was set afoot by the lathi charge of the police, all valour was held at bay and turned back.

Rukmani was brushed aside by some desperate arm until she reeled and fell not far from where she had sat waiting for the Sahib. But she clung to the handle of the cage in which her parrot sat as she lay moaning in suppressed, helpless whispers.

The parrot fluttering furiously as though he was being strangled and called out shrilly:

'Rukmaniai! Ni Rukmaniai! *Ni tun kithe hain! Ni tun ki karni hain!'*

But the old woman, though concerned for him had turned in upon herself with a sudden dimness that seemed to be creeping upon her.

After the crowd had been cleared, and the dust settled, the gram seller was irritated by the parrot's constant cries into stirring from his perch. He was afraid that the old woman had expired. But as he came near her, the parrot called her more shrilly and she answered faintly, 'H*am, han son, han*', and the man knew that she was still alive. He lifted her up and found that her hands and arms were slightly grazed.

'Come and sit in the shade, mother,' he said. Acha, son, acha!' she moaned.

And she lifted the cage and proceeded towards the shade.

The parrot was a little reassured as he saw the gram-seller helping his mistress and he shrieked less shrilly.

'Come, my little winged one, I shall give you some gram to eat', the gram seller said to him.

'May you live long, son!' the old woman blessed the gram seller in a feeble, strained moanful voice.

'Rukmaniai ni Rukmaniai! *Tun kithe hain? Tun ki karni hain...?* the parrot called now in a slow measured voice.

'Han han, son, han my son... I don't know where I am! I don't know...'

9

The Gold Watch*

There was something about the smile of Mr. Acton, when he came over to Srijut Sudarshan Sharma's table, which betokened disaster. But as the Sahib had only said, "Mr. Sharma, I have brought something for you specially from London — you must come into my office on Monday and take it...", the poor old dispatch clerk could not surmise the real meaning of the General Manager's remark. The fact that Mr. Acton should come over to his table at all, fawn upon him and say what he had said was, of course, most flattering. For, very rarely did the head of the firm condescend to move down the corridor where the Indian staff of the distribution department of the great Marmalade Empire of Henry King & Co., worked. But that smile on Mr. Acton's face — specially as Mr. Acton's face! — specially as Mr. Action was not known to smile too much, being a morose, old Sahib, hard working, conscientious and a slave driver, famous as a shrewd businessman, so devoted to the job of spreading the monopoly of King's Marmalade, and sundry other products, that his wife had left him after a three month's spell of marriage and never returned to India,

---

* From *The Power of Darkness; and Other Stories.*

though no one quite knew whether she was separated or divorced from him or merely preferred to stay away. So the fact that Acton Sahib should smile was enough to give Srijut Sharma cause for thought. But then Srijut Sharma was, in spite of his nobility of soul and fundamental innocence, experienced enough in his study of the vague, detached race of the white Sahibs by now and clearly noticed the slight awkward curl of the upper lip, behind which the determined, tobacco-stained long teeth showed, for the briefest moment, a snarl suppressed, by the deliberation which Acton Sahib had brought to the whole operation of coming over and pronouncing those kind words. And what could be the reason for his having being singled out, from amongst the twenty-five odd members of the distribution department? In the usual way, he, the dispatch clerk, only received an occasional greeting, "Hello Sharma — how you getting on?" from the head of his own department, Mr. West; and twice or thrice a year he was called into the cubicle by West Sahib for a reprimand, because some letters or packets had gone astray; otherwise, he himself, being the incarnation of clock-work efficiency, and well-versed in the routine of his job, there was no occasion for any break in the monotony of that anonymous, smooth working Empire, so far at least as he was concerned. To be sure, there was the continual gossip of the clerks and the accountants, the bickerings and jealousies of the people above him, for grades and promotions and pay; but he, Sharma, had been employed twenty years ago, as a special favour, was not even a matriculate, but had picked up the work somehow, and though unwanted and constantly reprimanded by West Sahib in the first few years, had been retained because of the general legend of saintliness which he had acquired... he had five more years of service to do, because then he would be fifty-five, and the family-raising, *grhast,* portion of his life in the fourfold scheme, prescribed by religion, finished, he hoped to retire to his home town Jullunder, where his father still ran the confectioner's shop off the Mall Road.

"And what did Acton Sahib have to say to you, Mr. Sharma?" asked Miss violet Dixon, the plain snub-nosed Anglo Indian typist in her singsong voice.

Being an old family man of fifty, who had grayed prematurely, she considered herself safe enough with this 'gentleman' and freely conversed with him, specially during the lunch hour, while she considered almost everyone else as having only one goal in life — to sleep with her.

'Han', he said, 'He has brought something for me from England', Srijut Sharma answered.

"There are such pretty things in U.K." she said.

'My! I wish, I could go there! My sister is there, you know! Married!...'

She had told Sharma all these things before. So he was not interested. Specially today, because all his thoughts were concentrated on the inner meaning of Mr. Acton's sudden visitation and the ambivalent smile.

'Well, half day today, I am off;, said Violet and moved away with the peculiar snobbish agility of the Mem Sahib she affected to be.

Srijut Sharma stared at her blankly, though taking in her regular form into his subconscious with more than the old uncle's interest he had always pretended to take in her. It was only her snub nose, like that of surpnaka, the sister of the demon king Ravana, that stood in the way of her being married, he felt sure, for otherwise she had a tolerable figure. But he lowered his eyes as soon as the thought of Miss Dixon's body began to simmer in the cauldron of his inner life; because, as a good Hindu, every woman, apart from the wife, was to him a mother or a sister. And his obsession about the meaning of Acton Sahib's words returned, from the pent up curiosity, with greater force now that he realised the vastness of the space of time during which he would have to wait in suspense before knowing what the boss had brought for him and why.

He took up his faded sola topee, which was, apart from the bush shirt and trousers, one of the few concessions to modernity which he had made throughout his life as a good Brahmin, got up from his chair, beckoned Dugdu sepoy from the verandah on his way out and asked.

"Has Acton Sahib gone, you know?"

"Abhi Sahib in lift going down," Dugdu said.

Srijut Sharma made quickly for the stairs and, throwing all caution about slipping on the polished marble steps to the winds, hurtled down. There were three floors below him and he began to sweat, both through fear of missing the Sahib and the heat of mid-April.

As he got to the ground floor, he saw Acton Sahib already going out of the door.

It was now or never.

Srijut Sharma rushed out. But he was conscious that

quite a few employers of the firm would be coming out of the two lifts and he might be seen talking to the Sahib. And that was not done — outside the office. The Sahibs belonged to their private worlds, where no intrusion was tolerated, for they refuse to listen to pleas of advancement through improper channels.

Mr. Acton's uniformed driver opened the door of the polished Buick and the Sahib sat down, spreading the shadow of grimness all around him.

Srijut Sharma hesitated, for the demeanour of the Goanese chauffeur was frightening.

By now the driver had smartly shut the back door of the car and was proceeding to his seat.

That was his only chance.

Taking off his hat, he rushed up to the window of the car, and rudely thrust his head into the presence of Mr. Acton.

Luckily for him, the Sahib did not brush him aside, but smiled a broader smile than that of a few minutes ago and said: 'You want to know, what I have brought for you -— well, it is a gold watch with an inscription in it... See me Monday morning...' The Sahib's initiative in anticipating his question threw Srijut Sharma further off his balance. The sweat poured down from his forehead, even as he mumbled: 'Thank You, Sir, thank you...'

'Chalo, driver!' Sahib ordered.

And the chauffeur turned and looked hard at Srijut Sharma.

The dispatch clerk withdrew' with a sheepish, abject smile

on his face and stood, hat in left hand, the right hand raised to his forehead in the attitude of a nearly military salute.

The motor car moved off.

But Srijut Sharma still stood, as though he had been struck dumb. He was neither happy nor sad at this moment. Only numbed by the shock of surprise. Why should he be singled out from the whole distribution department of Henry King & Co., for the privilege of the gift of a gold watch! He had done nothing brave that he could remember.' A gold watch, with an inscription in it!' Oh, he knew, now: the intuitive truth rose inside him: The Sahib wanted him to retire.

The revelation rose to the surface of his awareness from the deep obsessive fear, which had possessed him for nearly half an hour, and his heart began to palpitate against his will; and the sweat sozzled his body.

He reeled a little, then adjusted himself and got on to the pavement, looking after the car, which had already turned the corner into Nicol Road.

He turned and began to walk towards Victoria Terminus station. From there he had to take his train to Thana, thirty miles out where he had resided, for cheapness, almost all the years he had been in Bombay. His steps were heavy, for he was reasonably sure now that he would get notice of retirement on Monday. He tried to think of some other possible reason why the Sahib may have decided to give him the gift of a gold watch with an inscription. There was no other explanation. His doom was sealed. What would he say to his wife? And his son had still not passed his matric. How would he support the family? The provident fund would not amount to very much specially in these days of rising prices.

He felt a pull at his heart. He paused for breath and tried to call himself. The blood pressure! Or was it merely wind? He must not get into a panic at any cost. He steadied his gait and walked along, muttering to himself, 'Shanti! Shanti! Shanti!' as though the very incantation of the formula of peace would restore his calm and equanimity.

During the weekend, Srijut Sharma was able to conceal his panic and confusion behind the facade of an exaggerated bonhomie with the skill of an accomplished natural actor. On Saturday night he went with wife and son to see Professor Ram's Circus, which was performing opposite the Portuguese Church; and he got up later than usual on Sunday morning; spent a little longer on his prayers, but seemed normal enough on the surface.

Only, he ate very little of the gala meal of the rice-kichri put before him by his wife and seemed lost in thought for a few moments at a time. And his illiterate but shrewd wife noticed that there was something on his mind.

'Thou has not eaten at all today,' she said, as he had left the tasty papadum and the mango pickle untouched. 'Look at Hari! He has left nothing in his thali!'

'Hoon,' he answered abstractedly. And, then realising he might be found out for the worried, unhappy man he was, he tried to bluff her. 'As a matter of fact, I was thinking of some happy news that the Sahib gave me yesterday: He said, he brought a gold watch as a gift for me from Vilayat...'

'Then Papaji give me the silver watch, which you are using

now,' said Hari his young son impetuously. 'I have no watch at all and I am always late everywhere.'

'Not so impatient, son!' counselled Hari's mother. 'Let your father get the gold watch first and then — he will surely give you his silver watch.'

In the ordinary way, Srijut Sudarshan Sharma would have endorsed his wife's sentiments. But today, he felt that, on the face of it, his son's demand was justified. How should Hari know that the silver watch, and the gold watch, and a gold ring, would be all the jewellery he, the father, would have for security against hard days if the gold watch was, as he prognosticated, only a token being offered by the firm to sugarcoat the bitter pill they would ask him to swallow — retirement five years before the appointed time. He hesitated, then lifted his head, smiled at his son and said:

'Acha, Kaka, you can have my silver watch...'

'Can I have it, really, Papaji-Hurray!' the boy shouted, rushing away to fetch the watch from his father's pocket. 'Give it to me now, today!'

'Vay son, you are so selfish!' his mother exclaimed. For, with the peculiar sensitiveness of the woman she had surmised from the manner in which, her husband had hung his head down and then tried to smile as he lifted his face to his son, that the father of Hari was upset inside him, or at least not in his usual mood of accepting life evenly, accompanying this acceptance with the pious invocation — 'Shanti! Shanti!'

Hari brought the silver watch, adjusted it to his left ear to see if it ticked, and happy in the possession of it, capered a little caper.

Srijut Shanna did not say anything, but pushing his thali away, got up to wash his hands.

The next day it happened as Srijut Sharma had anticipated.

He went in to see Mr. Acton as soon as the Sahib came in, for the suspense of the weekend had mounted to a crescendo by Monday morning and he had been 'trembling with trepidation, pale and completely unsure of himself. The General Manager called him in immediately the peon Dugdu presented the little slip with the dispatch clerk's name on it.

'Please, sit down, said Mr. Acton, lifting his grey-haired head from the papers before him. And then, pulling his keys from his trousers' pocket by the gold chain to which they were adjusted, he opened a drawer and fetched out what Sharma thought was a beautiful red case.

'Mr. Sharma, you have been a loyal friend of this firm for many years — and you know, your loyalty has been your greatest asset here — because...er... Otherwise, we could have got someone, with better qualifications to do your work!... Now... we are thinking of increasing the efficiency of the business all round!... And, we, feel that you would also like, at your age, to retire to your native Punjab... So, as a token of our appreciation for your loyalty to Henry King & Co., we are presenting you this gold watch...' and he pushed the red case towards him.

'Srijut Sharma began to speak, but though his mouth opened, he could not go on. 'I am fifty years old,' he wanted to say, 'And I still have five years to go.' His facial muscles seemed to contract, his eyes were dimmed with the fumes of frustration and bitterness, his forehead was covered with sweat. At least, they might have made a little ceremony of the presentation, he could not even utter the words: 'Thank you, Sir!'

'Of course, you will also have your provident fund and one month's leave with pay before you retire...'

Again, Srijut Sharma tried to voice his inner protest in words which would convey his meaning without seeming to be disloyal, for he did not want to obliterate the one concession the Sahib had made to the whole record of his service with his firm. It was just likely that Mr. Acton may remind him of his failings as a despatch clerk if he should so much as indicate that he was unamenable to the suggestion made by the Sahib on behalf of Henry King & Co.

'Look at the watch — it has an inscription in it which will please you,' said Mr. Acton, to get over the embarrassment of the tension created by the silence of the despatch clerk.

These words hypnotised Sharma and, stretching his hands across the large table, he reached out for the gift.

Mr. Acton noticed the unsureness of his hand and pushed it gently forward.

Srijut Sharma picked up the red box, but, in his eagerness to follow the Sahib's behests, dropped it, even as he had held it aloft and tried to open it.

The Sahib's face was livid as he picked up the box and hurriedly opened it. Then, lifting the watch from its socket, he wound it and applied it to his' ear. It was ticking. He turned it round and showed the inscription to the dispatch clerk.

Srijut Sharma put both his hands out, more steadily this time, and took the gift in the manner in which a beggar receives alms. he brought the glistening object within the orbit of his eyes, but they were dimmed to smile, however, and, then with a great heave of his head, which rocked his body from side to side, he pronounced the words:

'Thank you, Sir...'

Mr. Acton got up, took the gold watch from Srijut Sharma's hands and put it back in the socket of the red case. Then he stretched his right hand towards the despatch clerk, with a brisk shake-hand gesture and offered the case to him with his left hand.

Srijut Sharma instinctively took the Sahib's right hand gratefully in his two sweating hands and opened the palms out to receive the case.

'Good luck, Sharma,' Mr. Acton said, 'Come and see me after your leave is over. And when your son matriculates let me know if I can do something for him...'

Dumb, and with bent head, the fumes of his violent emotions rising above the mouth which could have expressed them, he withdrew in the abject manner of his ancestors going out of the presence of feudal lords.

Mr. Acton saw the danger to the watch and went ahead to open the door, so that the clerk could go out without knocking his head against the door or fall down.

As Srijut Sharma emerged from the General Manager's office, involuntary tears flowed from his eyes and his lower lip fell in a pout that somehow controlled him from breaking down completely.

The eyes of the whole office staff were on him.

In a moment, a few of the men clustered around his person.

One of them took the case from his hands, opened it and read the inscription out aloud:

"In appreciation of the loyal service of Mr. Sharma to Henry King & Co., on his retirement..."

The curiosity of his colleagues became a little less enthusiastic as the watch passed from hand to hand.

Unable to stand, because of the wave of dizziness that swirled in his head, Srijut Sudarshan Sharma sat down on his chair, with his head hidden in his hands and allowed the tears to roll down. One of his colleagues, Mr. Banaji, the accountant, patted his back understandingly. But the pity was too much for him.

"To be sure, Seth Makhanji, the new partner has a relation, to fill Sharma's position,' another said.

'No no,' another refuted him. 'No one is required to kill himself with work in our big concern... We are given the Sunday off'! And a fat pension years beyond it is due. The bosses are full of love for us!...

'Damn fine gold watch, but it does not go!' said Sriraman, the typist.

Mr. Banaji took the watch from Sriraman and, putting it in the case, placed it before Srijut Sharma and he signalled to the others to move away.

As Srijut Sharma realised that his colleagues had drifted

away, he lifted his morose head, took the case, as well as his hat, and began to walk away.

Mr. Banaji saw him off to the door, his hands on Sharma's back.

'Sahibji,' the Parsi accountant said, as the lift came up and the liftman took Srijut Sharma in.

On the way home Srijut Sharma found that the gold watch only went when it was shaken. Obviously, some delicate part had broken when he had dropped it on Mr. Acton's table. He would get it mended, but he must save all the cash he could get hold of and not go spending it on the luxury of having a watch repaired now. He shouldn't have been weak with his son and given him his old silver watch. But as there would be no office to go to any more, he would not need to look at the time very much, specially in Jullunder, where time just stood still and no one bothered about keeping appointments.

10

Old Bapu*

They say, in our parts, that, at the solemn moment of death, even when death is sudden, every man sees the whole of his past underneath his skull.

Old Bapu fancied, as he walked along towards the Gurgaon bazar that his end had come. And, as though by the power of this suggestion, the various worlds rose behind his head, way back in the distance of time, rather like balls of heat wrapped in mist, projections of the omnipotent Sun that shone overhead, veiled and blurred by the haze of memory...

The city was still a mile away, and the flesh of his feet burnt where it touched the new hot metalled road through the holes in the shoes. And the sweat poured down across the furrows on his face, specially through the two sharp channels which stretched from the nose towards the chin, like rivulets flooding a fallow field.

... A bluish simmer flickered across his vision of the houses ahead.

As though compelled by the discomfort of slogging on

* From *The Power of Darkness and Other Stories.*

foot and the weakness in his joints after the seven miles tread form Shikohpur, he felt his body evaporating, and his soul in the state of that lightness which disclosed the saga of his past life, going round and round in his cranium. And as he felt near enough to exhaustion and death, and yet did not want to die ('May Ishwar banish such a thought from my head,' he prayed), the agitation of his nerves produced the aberration of a phantasma, like the red starts over a toothache...

'I am not old, he said to himself in the silent colloquy of his soul with his body. 'The boys call me Old Bapu because I am older than them... The caste Hindu urchins have no respect for the untouchable elders anyhow. And their fathers want to throw everyone of us into the garbage pit to use as manure for better harvests... But I do not want to die... Hey Ishwar!'

The saga of his life forced itself into his head, in spite of his protests, in several minute details, bits of memories entangled with the awkward drone of heat overhead, drumming into his ears.

He was a child, sitting by the revolving spinning wheel of his mother, disturbing the iron needle because she would not get up and give him the stale bread and pickle... Little specks of wool arose from the cotton in her hand, soft as the sight which she uttered in despair at his mischief — or was it because there was no roti in the basket inside?... And then she awoke from the trance of her eyes rivetted on the thread of the *takla* and said: 'Acha, wah, tiny, I will go and borrow some food for you from the mother of Ram Dutt...' And while she was gone, and he played about with the spinning wheel, against her strict injunctions, a rat gnawing in his belly...'

Lighter than air, his body proceeded on the way to

Gurgaon bazar flitting into a cloud of unknowing. He walked almost with his eyes closed, seeing himself as a small boy singing a song, against the counterpoint of the wheel of well, as he drove the bullocks round and round... And the big boys came and pulled his slight frame from the seat and began to take a ride on the shaft. And, as he sought, with his tiny hands, to grip them, they thrust him away and threw him into the well, where he shrieked in panic, holding on to the chain of earthen vessels while they all ran away, and he slowly climbed up, exhausted and dying...

Drifting from that early death into life, he felt he could ward off the present feeling of weakness in his limbs, and, perhaps, he would be lucky, with at least half a day's work.

'Stay with me son; when you go from me I shall die!' he heard his mother's words beckon from the mythical memories of his adolescence. 'Your father went soon after you were born, and you will have no one after I am gone...' And he recalled that in his eagerness to work in the fields, and to become a tall man and not remain the small creature he was, he had gone away that afternoon, and then he had come home to find his mother dead... His spirit tried to fly away from the ugly thought of his betrayal of her, but its wings were rooted in his coarse little body, and in spite of a violent cough, which he excited in his throat, even as he spat on the dust a globule of phlegm, the soul held the vision of his mother's dead face, eyes dilated and the teeth showing in the terror dark of their hut...

'May Ishwar keep her soul in heaven!' he prayed. And, as though by magic, his treason was forgotten in the next few footsteps...

But even as he mopped the sweat off his face with the forepaws of his right hand, the scales seemed to lift from his eyes and his soul was face to face with the forepaws of his right hand, and then with a monster his Uncle Dandu Ram, who shouted: 'I am tired of you! Good for nothing scoundrel! Everyone is tired of you! Inauspicious bastard! You cannot plough the fields well! Nor can you look after the cattle! Go and eat dung elsewhere — there is no food for you in my house'.

The bushes on the roadside exhuded the same smell in the parched heat, which had come from the clumps of grass amid the mound and hollows of Shikhopur where he had wandered, half crazy with hunger and the beatings which the boys gave him, like birds of prey falling upon a weaker member of the flock... the cruelty of it! And the laceration of abuse and bitter words! And Dandu had taken his half bigha of land, saying, "You are an idiot, incapable of looking after it!'

The lava-mist of heat pressed down over his eyes and half shut them through the glare. The mood of his soul became more and more seraphic, accepting the vision of the crusts of black bread and lentils which he loved so much, after the work when he was engaged as field labourer by some prosperous Hindu farmer of the upper caste.

Only the anxiety of not getting work today began to gnaw into his being as the houses of Gurgaon loomed up fifty hands away.

A man mounted on a bicycle brushed past him from ahead after tinkling his bell furiously. And Bapu realised that he must be careful in town if he wanted to escape death.

The city was a labyrinth of jagged shops, tall houses and rutted roads, And waves of men coursed along the edges of the streets, receding, returning towards the hawkers, who sat with condiments and fruits and vegetables before them.

The broken asphalt attracted him. He had worked on road-making. Fetching stones and breaking them. So much cement was put down on certain roads that they never broke. But here, the contractors were paid, to make pavements hard, and to fill the ruts every season, for after every rainy season the ruts reappeared.

That was the work he had come to ask for.

Suddenly, he turned in the direction of the Model Town where the Sikh contractor, Ram Singh, lived.

In his heart there was an old cry of fear at the potential temper of this man, which had always cowed him down. His glance fell at his fingertips which had been blunted through hammering stones. The congealed flesh of corns at the ends of the fingers gave the effect of toughness and he felt strong to see them, knowing that he was capable of the hardest work... Distant, more distant seemed to grow the contractor's house with the courtyard, even though he had entered the Model Town, but his feet marched more briskly.

Sardar Ram Singh was sitting on a charpai under the neem tree, the bun of his hair a little loose from sleep.

Bapu joined his hands and stood looking at the god.

"Aoji Bapu!' the contractor said surlily breaking the edge of his taciturnity.

The vibration of each part of Ram Singh's face made

Bapu's soul shudder, and he could not speak.

'Ohe speak — What do you want!' Ram Singh asked, fanning himself with a hand fan.

The voice surged up in Bapu even as he breathed deeply to sigh. But the sound would not come out.

Ram Singh stared at him for a prolonged moment.

Bapu made a sign with his hands and opened his mouth to say: 'Work', 'Ohe ja ja, oldie! You can't work, with that frame of yours!... Doing half work for full pay!...Beside the rains have not yet abated. Don't be deceived by this sunshine... The big rains have yet to come!...

A low and horrible sound was in Bapu's belly, and he felt that his throat was being strangled by the serpent of Sweat that flowed down to his neck from the face. His lips twitched, and the tone of the contractor's words sounded like the news of doom in his ears. 'How old are you?' Ram Singh asked eyeing him with seemingly cynical indifference.

'The earthquake in Kangra — when it came, I was born!'

'The contractor was startled. He smiled, and surveying Bapu's frame said: 'About fifty years ago-but you look seventy. Life in our country is ebbing away The workmen seem to have no strength left. Look at you, two-legged donkey that you are! One of your legs seems to be 'shrivelled, while the other feeble one seems to be waiting to drag it on... All of us have become lame and go hopping, tottering and falling, wishing for the Sarkar to carry us forward. Comic and undignified and shameless!..'

'No land, no harvests!' Bapu said desperately.

'And —' And he stretched out his hand.

Acha, take this and go, the contractor ground the words and looked away, 'Let me rest. Take this...' He took a nickel piece and threw it at Bapu.

The labourer bent his eyes over his hands, joined them in supplication and gratitude and still stood.

'*Ja,* don't stand on my head!' Ram Singh shouted. The work on the roads will begin when the rains are over!'

Bapu was more frightened of his agony of frustration than of the contractor's words. He controlled the tears in his eyes and slid away on ambling feet.

The prolonged burbling of a beetle from the slime in a drain stirred a feeling of terrible self-pity in him. He wanted to drink some water to avoid breaking down. And, seeing a lone pan-biri stall, tucked away between the walls of the two different houses, a little further away, he headed towards it.

His eyes were almost closed his lips twitched against his will. And he was like a somnambulist, walking blindly towards some unknown goal. The fact that he had a nickel piece in his hands warded off the feeling of death that had pre-occupied him on the approach towards Gurgaon. Now, he only felt the precariousness of the dim future, in which his good or bad deeds would rotate in the inexorable rhythm of work and no work.

'Pani!' he said to the shopkeeper, joining his hands, first in greeting, then unfolding them as a cup.

The pan-biri wallah eyed him suspiciously, then relaxed in the face of the sun's merciless stare, and began to pour water into the stranger's cupped hands from a brass jug.

Bapu drank and belched his fill. Then he caressed his face with his moist hands and touched his eyes with the water on his fingertips. The cool touch of liquid seemed to revive him.

And, as though from some instinct for seeking reassurance, he looked into the mottled mirror that hung down from the pan-biri shop. He had not looked at himself in such a glass for years. He saw that his face was shrivelled up, lined with the wrinkles which had been sharpened by hard work in his youth, and many small lines criss-crossed the corners of his eyes, his forehead, his jowl and neck. And a greyish pallor covered the visage, more than the abject anxiety to please the contractor, rather like the colour of death which he had apprehended as he had walked along the road. The shock of the old fact disturbed him and he turned away from the mirror. 'About seventy years!' Ram Singh said. So he turned towards the mirror again.

'Oh *ja, ja,* ahead', said the pan-biri wallah. 'Don't break my glass by showing it your ugly old face!'

Old Bapu ambled along ahead, hoping to buy four annas worth of corn to sustain himself in the illusion of youth.

11

The Cobbler and the Machine*

Apart from the innocence of old age and youth, Saudagar, the cobbler of my village, and I shared in common a passion for the machine.

Saudagar, of course, was interested in only one machine, the small sewing-machine which the village tailor wielded very ostentatiously on the footboard of his cavernous shop before the gaping rustics, who had often travelled fifty miles from their homes in the hills to see it — a grimy, black hand-machine in a casket, decorated with a tracery of leaves in yellow paint, that nibbled at the yards of cloth like a slimy rat, at terrific speed. But I liked all kinds of machines which I saw in the town where I went to school every morning: the great big railway-engine, whose *phuff-phuff* I had learned to imitate when we played at trains at the recess hour: the phonograph from which I hoped to hear my own voice one day; the motor-car in which my father was given a lift by Lalla Sain Das when there was an election; the push-bike on which our second

* From *The Barber s Trade Union and Other Stories.*

master came to school from his bungalow; the intricate mass of wheels and pistons which lay hiccuping in the power house at the junction of the two canals; and the roaring monsters of iron and steel that converted the cotton and wool of our village into cloth at the Dhariwal mills. And even of sewing-machines I had seen at least two varieties other than the one that Saudagar knew, and yet a third-a pedal-machine, adjusted to a chair with a leather belt across it, to which I used to see Baha-ud-din, the tailor in the main bazaar in the town, glued all day, and a similar upright contraption on which one of the employees in the Bhalla shoe shop sat sewing boots.

'Uncle Saudagar,' I said to the cobbler one day as I sat idly at the door of his dark straw hut while he stared across the street at Bhagirath, the tailor, revolving the handle of his sewing-machine with amazing alacrity. 'Do you know, you waste so much of your time sewing pieces of leather to the soles of people's shoes and then they complain that you don't sew them well and that the water gets into them? Why, you could have a machine like Bhagirath's, even superior, with a seat attached to it like the chairs the Sahibs sit on. I have seen a man in the Bhalla shoe shop sewing boots on one.'

'Is there a machine like that, son?' said Saudagar incredulously, and yet vaguely convinced, as he had been for months since the tailor brought his casket machine, that there must be a contrivance for sewing leather as there was one for sewing cloth.

'Yes, uncle,' I said enthusiastically, for to me all machines were still toys and play things, rather than 'chariots — which men could ride.' 'There are wonderful machines in the town if only you will go and see, but you never stir out of this hovel.

Didn't you go to see the great exhibition at Lahore? My father tells me there was a great big boot there all sewn by machine in which people could play hide-and-seek.' I had seen the wonders of science in the school laboratory and the marvels in the streets of the town and wished rather too eagerly that they could come to my village, so convinced was I of the superiority of modernity over the old ways of the countryside.

'Well, son,' said the old man kindly, 'I have heard that there is a machine which can do the work of my hand, but I have never seen it. Ever since I saw the ready-made saddles, reins and collars in the stables of Thakur Mahan Chand, I knew they were made by a defter hand than that of man. And when the son of the landlord sent me the black leather boots which he bought in town to mend, I knew that they couldn't have been sewn by any human being. And truly, I have been looking at Bhagirath's sewing-machine and wondering if there is a similar contraption for sewing shoes. But I am old and I have not been to town these ten years. So I have not seen what this machine looks like. One day I must make a trip to see it. But of course, I am too poor ever to be able to buy it. And perhaps God would curse my fingers and those of my pupils, and make them incapable of sewing at all, if I began to use this machine.'

'But, Uncle Saudagar,' I said, I tell you, you will like this machine if you see it. And you will look like a Sahib sitting on the chair which is adjusted to it. You will only need a basket-hat to complete your life and you will begin to eat and drink on a raised platform automatically. I wish my mother would let me convert that broken pitcher we have into a chair and I could use the manger of the cows for a table always.'

'I am an outcast, son,' Saudagar said. 'How can I presume to eat like the Sahibs or be like them? And won't people laugh at me if they see me seated in a chair, sewing shoes?'

'But these people are fools, Uncle,' I said. 'They regard the Sahibs as outcasts, too, even though the Sahibs are clean. And these rustics have no idea of modern times. They are old fogies with jungly habits. They are oxen. They have no idea of the new life.'

'Yes, son, perhaps you are right,' said the old cobbler. 'God has created iron in the mountains. I suppose He meant us to make machines with it.'

'I have got a beautiful bolt I found in the playground, Uncle,' I said. 'I will show it to you, if you like.'

'I would like to see it, son,' said Saudagar indulgently. 'Now run along and go home. Your father might come this way and abuse you for wasting your time sitting in an outcast's shop. Run along and play with your fellows.'

'I will also bring you a picture of the sewing-machine, if you like, Uncle', I said, making an overture of friendship so as to win more easily the privilege of fidgeting round the cobbler's shop, for ordinarily he discouraged children from flocking round the door of his hovel and robbing his dim eyes of the little natural light that trickled through the aperture of the door.

'All right,' he said. 'All right, son. You must show me a picture if you can, though I don't know what use it is to show a man the likeness of a bunch of grapes when he will never be able to eat the fruit.'

But the spark that had failed to kindle a devouring flame in the heart of old Saudagar lit my flesh with the warmth of a new delight, for the echo of the old cobbler of my village handling a new machine reverberated in my brain like the voice of a wish that had become father to the thought. I ran towards home as if I were possessed by more than a love of the new toy that would be Saudagar's machine. I had a feeling that there might come to be in my village the atmosphere of a splendid, gorgeous wonder-house, in which great big iron frames, with a thousand screws and knobs assembled through the ingenuity of a man like my science master, created the power to achieve miracles.

I persuaded my class-fellows when we were coming home from school the next day to climb a high wall near the Railway Station and pull off a poster which showed an English woman, with a bun on the top of her head, wielding a Singer sewing-machine embossed on a steel plate in the shape of the letter S. And I brought it to Saudagar.

'This, Uncle,' I said, 'Is the kind of machine which I told you, you should have. Only this is for sewing cloth. But, the one for sewing leather which the man in the Bhalla shoe shop plies is like it in appearance, except that it has a thicker needle.'

The old cobbler looked at the picture in wide-eyed wonder. I could see from the loving way in which he passed his hand over the surface of the steel that his imagination had caught fire from the picture of the sewing-machine, bigger than Bhagirath's which seemed to make him firmly believe in the existence of a similar machine for sewing leather though he hadn't seen it.

And so charmed was he by the novelty of the instrument of which I had shown him the picture, that he asked us to bring the steel plate which we had stolen into his shop and leave it there for a decoration. And he gave us a piece each as compensation for our trouble.

It seemed to me that he had not kept the advertisement for the Singer sewing-machine merely for decorative purposes but because he wanted to see the likeness of the object which he had set his heart on buying one day. And my feeling was confirmed by the fact that whenever I went to his hovel now he would always say something about the shape of the needle in the picture not being quite clear, and of his inability to understand how one could get into the habit of pressing the pedal with the feet while one was sewing something on top.

'And the stool seems too small,' he said. 'It may be all right for the "lendis" to sit on, but how will such a crude old bottom as mine balance on it?'

'Don't you care,' I said, with an emphasis that gained weight from the earnestness and zeal I felt at the prospect of seeing the cobbler of my village achieve the dexterity of the man in the Bhalla shoe shop. 'A little practice and you will learn to wield it better than anyone else, and as for your old posterior, why, I have seen the heavy-bottomed Mem Sahib, who is the wife of the City Engineer, balanced on a stool like that in the verandah of her bungalow, as if she were seated on a comfortable horse."

A look of wonder lit his dim eyes and, glancing at me with the tenderness of humility, he traced the curves of the steel plate on the picture of the machine printed in black-and-white against the green. And then he would close his eyes and, smiling, shake his head as if he were surcharged with the ecstasy of a knowledge in the hollows of his brain where phantasmagoric visions of himself at work on the new machine swirled in a mad delirium, the edges of enchanting top-boots, splendid, well-polished shoes, and strong-soled country shoes creating and destroying each other in an irrelevant disorder.

'But anyhow, the trouble is, son, where am I to get the money to buy the machine?' the old man would then say with a sigh, and continue: 'I don't know how I shall get it, and where it is to be got even if I had the money, which I shall never have.'

The grim sagacity of his practical argument defeated my intelligence, for I had no idea how many rupees the machine cost and where Saudagar was to get the money, but, of course, the address of the Singer Sewing Machine Company, England, was printed at the bottom of the picture, and I speculated that if that company manufactured sewing-machines for cloth, surely they made those for sewing leather, and I said: it is made in Vilayat, and can be had from there, or perhaps through a commission agent in Lahore or Bombay, if not in our district.'

'Vilayat is very far away', Saudagar. said, 'And I shall never cross the seven seas even when I go to Heaven, because I have-not done enough good deeds to earn the privilege of being able to travel in my next life. As for Lahore and Bombay, if anyone is going there from our parts we will make inquiries.

But for days and weeks and months no one from our parts was going to Lahore Delhi, or Bombay, and I hugged the desperate enthusiasm for Saudagar's sewing-machine in my heart till the cool waters of a placid existence had washed off the bright edges of my dreams. I went to see the cobbler as usual in the afternoons, but the topic of the machine was seldom mentioned, and instead the old man bent over the shoes he was mending, brushed his beard, and, with a mischievous light in his eyes, told me a story about some ogre or wild animal, or the witchery of an old maiden who died without ever being married.

One day, however, when I was waiting at the usual hour for my friends to emerge from their homes to play in a maidan near Saudagar's house, he called me and, 'with a weird chuckle that rose above the curve of his usual silence of a madman, he said: 'Come here, son, and guess what has happened.'

'What is it, then?' I asked, at first completely taken aback but then warming to the happy glare in his eyes with a sensation that the cause of Saudagar's sudden happiness was somehow connected with our project about the machine.

'You know, son, that Lalla Sain Das, the notary and cotton dealer, has gone to vilayat on business. Well, he asked me to make him some gold-worked shoes to give as present to his clients beyond the seas. When he came to collect them he asked me politely whether he could do something for me while he was away. And I asked him to fetch a machine for sewing leather. He was very kind and said he would bring the machine most willingly. And what is more, that since he knew I was a poor man who couldn't pay him for the thing at once, he would buy the machine at his own expense and let me use it and pay for it by and by exactly as if it were a loan with a small interest attached to it. Now I have had this letter from the rail office and the Munshi read it and he says that it is the voucher for the sewing-machine which Lalla Sain Das has sent from Vilayat and which is lying in the railway godown. So, please

God, I shall have the machine after all. I am going to distribute sugar-plums among the brotherhood to celebrate the auspicious occasion when the machine comes, and I will make you a pair of Angrezi boots, since it was really you who told me about it.

I clapped my hands with joy, breathed some breaths quickly, and stimulated my being with shouts of 'Marvellous! Marvellous!' And, either because I easily whipped myself into a kind of elemental buoyancy, or because it was the natural colour of my temperament, I danced in my mind to the cadence of a rhythm I could feel in the working of the machine, in its contours, in its dainty, intricate contrivances, its highly ingenious purpose, in the miracle it was to me, an architecture embodying mysteries which not only represented the exact formula of science and mathematics, but was the magnificent toy, the plaything. And, of course, Saudagar's offer of a pair of Angrezi boots, such as I had been persuading my father to buy for me for years, made me hysterically happy, for I felt that I could rise in the estimation of all my fellows by possessing footwear which was worn only by the Sahib and the rich folk.

'When will you actually get the machine Uncle?' I asked eagerly.

'I shall go and get it tomorrow, son,' he said. 'It is after eleven years that I am going to town.'

'If you are in town, go and get the advice of the cobbler in the Bhalla shoe shop, as to how to work it.'

'That is a good idea,' Saudagar said. 'Yes, I will do that. And since you have been so good to me, child, I shall take your measurements now and start sewing your shoes first on the machine.'

I would have stayed and talked about the possibilities of the new wonder to Saudagar if my friends had not been calling incessantly, but that afternoon I was too preoccupied by my ardour to put my heart into playing Kabadi, and I couldn't sleep in the night for the sheer excitement of sharing the glory of having inspired the old cobbler. In the morning I ran along to school bound up in the curves of a rich stillness, the radiant exultation of a child whose fantastic dreams have, for the first time, achieved the guise of visible truths. And all day I was full of mischief the tingling shadow of an ingrown largeness in my being played havoc with every mundane fact, the vastness of the creator laughed at people, and the depths of a realised truth mocked at impossibilities.

Off I went to Saudagar's shop immediately after I returned from school and, true as the very colour of my dream, even truer because harder, the sewing-machine was before me, with the old cobbler seated on the stool adjusted to it, sewing a piece of leather, with beads of perspiration on his forehead, as his two pupils, and a number of other people of low and high castes crowded into the hovel to see the wizardry.

'Come, son,' Saudagar said, lifting his eyes and breathing a mouthful of stale breath. 'This is the upper part of the boots I am going to sew for you, since you must have the first-fruits of my acquisition.

I smiled awkwardly and then felt a sudden urge to touch the wonderful new thing which was exactly like the sewing-machine of which I had brought Saudagar the picture, except that it had no casket to enclose the upper part, but an anvil into which the needle darted like a shaft, probing the leather in between with the cotton in its eye. But I curbed my childish desire as, just then, Saudagar brushed aside the crowd which was clamouring to touch it, and I only asked: 'When will my shoes be ready, Uncle?'

'You shall have them by and by,' Saudagar said. 'I will sew them at any odd times I get, because all the rest of my time must be devoted to turning out enough work to pay off the debt I owe on the machine to Lalla Sain Das, who is coming back tomorrow.'

My visits to the cobbler's shop became more frequent since I could always excuse myself to my parents by saying that I was going to the outcast's quarter to see how the boots that Saudagar had promised to make me were getting on. And as my old Indian shoes made of crude hide were wearing out and my parents would have had to buy me a new pair if Saudagar had not offered me the gift, I was allowed to go and waste as much time as I liked.

Saudagar had added a pattern of stitches to the shoes he intended for me during the first few days, but then he had hung them up as a sample on the door of his hut, and was mainly busy turning out Indian shoes by the dozen to defray the sum of one thousand rupees, which Sain Das had declared to be the cost of the machine plus freightage and taxes. Every time I went the old man would pick up the sample and contemplate it with an air of absorption and say: 'Well, son, I believe I shall begin to sew the lining to them next week, and then I must send Majitha to get some leather for the soles and heels. Or would you like rubber soles instead?'

'No, I want leather soles and rubber heels, Uncle,' I said,

swinging from the first disappointment of seeing the shoes no further advanced to a sudden excitement.

'You, can't have both, son,' Saudagar would say kindly. 'I want to set the fashion,' I replied.

'But, son, let me make you an ordinary pair first,' said the old man,' 'And then later —'

'When will they be ready?' I would ask impatiently. 'Tomorrow, by the grace of God, tomorrow I shall do something to them...'

But tomorrow and tomorrow and tomorrow came and went, and as my old Indian shoes were completely worn out and discarded, I trudged barefoot to and from school, and cursed both my parents for not buying me a new pair of Angrezi shoes and Saudagar for not completing the pair he had promised me.

I couldn't realise that my parents were poor and could not afford to buy me a pair of English boots, and I was too obstinate to accept a cheap pair of Indian shoes. But Saudagar's work was pledged to Lalla Sain Das for the money the cobbler had borrowed to buy the machine, and I was disgusted.

'Let me buy a good pair of shoes like your old one's my mother said.

'No, I replied stubbornly. 'I want English shoes and you needn't bother because Saudagar is making them for me.'

"Never trust a washerman's promise, nor a goldsmith's nor a cobbler's," she quoted the proverb.

But mine was the faith that would have moved mountains

but for the fact that an act of God intervened. Saudagar, the old cobbler, fell ill and was unable to work for days, and when he got up from his illness he had to clear arrears of debt and work so hard on his ordinary job that he had no time left even to think of the shoes he had so lovingly cut and on which he had sewn the first stitches. And considering that he had not been able to pay up even the arrears of interest on the cost of the machine, there was little prospect of his ever completing the job for me.

I looked at the old man bending over the machine and working patiently as the sweat poured from his face on to his neck and then on to the earth, and I felt constrained not to trouble him with my demands. And the mixture of resentment and pity I felt for the old man became transformed into feeling of hate for the machine, for, as it stood hard, hard and unbending, it seemed to have become a barrier between Saudagar and me and the thing which had emphasized his self-interest so that he never seemed to put a stitch on anyone's shoes without insisting on being paid for it. And as he sat tied to the chariot wheels of doom, he also began to be more and more reticent, as if he were turning in upon himself to drink his own blood in the silent places of his heart, and the illumination of his natural manner disappeared behind a pale, shadowy face that was always dirty and grimy with a layer of scum on the sweat covered beard. And still the sample shoes of English design meant for me stood unfinished, while he and his assistants worked furiously to produce enough to pay off the debt on the machine.

I shook the roots of hope from their foundation in my heart and rarely visited Saudagar's shop, thinking he would call me one day when the remorse of his unfulfilled promise had prompted him to finish making my boots.

But that day never came, for worn out by the fatigue of producing many more shoes than he had ever sewn to pay off his debt, drained of his life-blood by the sweat that was always pouring off his body, he fell stone dead one evening as he recited the devotional verse:

'The days of your life are ending

And you have not made your accounts with God.'

In the amorphous desert of my familiar thoughts I felt the pain of silent guilt, as I knew that I had to some extent been the cause of his death. If only I had known then that it was not enough for Saudagar and his pupils to love the machine and work it, but to own it, I could have defied the verdict of the village which said that Saudagar was killed by the devil disguised in the image of the sewing-machine.

Part III

THE SOCIAL SCENE

12

The Power of Darkness*

In the autumn of last year, I visited Mangal, the site for the new dam that has harnessed the course of one of the oldest waters of the land of five rivers. The sun, seemed, in the afternoons, to set fire to the surface of the new canals and made the earth look like beaten gold. And the pylons seemed to speak to the sky. And, seeing the wonder of it all, the ejaculation came spontaneously from my lips, in the homely Punjabi tongue; 'In the jungle has arisen this Mangal!' My speech fell on the ears of an electrician of the nearby powerhouse. And, as he opened his mouth and uttered his dictum, in the northern refugee accent, 'Green shoots will soon stand with their roots moistened by this nectar', I surmised from the lilt in his voice that he was somewhat by way of being a poet. A little later, I heard him hum a tune from our famous epic, Hir and Ranjha. And, compelled by nostalgia, I asked him to sing again. Instead, he began to tell me the story of Mangal. That tale is told here in the words of Bali the

---

* From *The Power of Darkness and Other Stories.*

Bard, (for that was his name, I discovered), almost he told it to me. And it seems, that the lyrical manner of his telling almost achieves the dramatic tension necessary to a modem story, mastering the laws of space and time.

'Of all the gods and goddesses of our country, Shakti is the most supreme. To be sure, everything is Shakti, soul and body, earth and sky and the waters that flow from their union...'

'But how were the villages of Kamli to know this truth? For when the gloom of madness falls upon the soul, so that it turns to rend and destroy its nearest and dearest, when the light of dread it be a man, woman or child, then who can find in the maleficent presence of fear, his chiefest good?

'And, as the power of darkness blurs the outline of things around us, seeming to free us from the rule of daylight, but really consigning us to hell, when we ourselves beckon the god of the netherworld Yama, and his *doots,* we have to close our eyes in order to explore our inner selves, and rescue, from the silences, the strength to face a future which we cannot understand...

'Our profoundest truth today, brother, consists in this: That we have a capacity for great works. And if I, Bali, know anything about anything, since I know much about electricity, then these big works are organised schemes, in which the sparks are lit in order to free men from their fetters, to enable them to surpass themselves, and to give all that they have and what they acquire to their children.

'But how can one show this spirit of light to the dark-minded and the dead in heart?'

"If it exists, they said, "show it to us! How can your electricity vie with Kamli, the mother, after whom our village is named? This giant monster of cement and steel, which you are helping to build in your dam, is an insult offered to our ancient goddess! For ages she has directed the courses of the sun, the moon and the stars. And every part of our land is imbued with the spirit of Kamli. And we have had good harvests, plentiful ones, until you refugees came and began to devour our stocks, snatching bread from the mouths of our children! And now those, who are in authority, declare that our village of Kamli is to be submerged in the artificial lake they are constructing. And they want us to move away, before the water fills this construction of the iron age and the canals begin to flow...! To be sure they have given us some compensation and some fallow land, near Chandigarh, where hey have built barrack-like structures on the sites where the goddess Chandi manifested herself for the first time when she walked down form the high peaks of the Daula Dar to the plains! Ruffians and Scoundrels! Drunk with power! Respecting neither religion nor the gods. And to think that the Prime Minister of this faithless country is himself a Brahmin. Look, folks darkness has come!"

'And though the work proceeded on the huge dam, and the time seemed to come nearer, when the waters of the artificial lake, Mangal Sagar, were to submerge the little hamlet of Kamli, the villagers, who talked like this, would not move.'

'And thus a drama was enacted before our eyes, of which you may see the happy ending, but of which you do not know the various parts. Even I can detach myself today and talk of that grim struggle in an even voice, but those were solemn moments, brother, those moments when, for days, we were on the brink of death and destruction, and from which we emerged only because some transcended themselves...Only a few know that God does not fix the prices of grain, and that droughts can be avoided by making rain; but the worshippers of Kamli did not believe this and talked of fate and invoked the curses of the Goddess... In those moments of mortal agony, when the lips of these men only framed abuse and oaths and imprecations, I groaned many a time, the cry we utter in our deepest need," oh mother!"...

"Tell me, then, brother Bali, the story of this struggle," I interrupted.

The bard closed his eyes for a moment as though he was encompassing all the solemn moments of death, all the moment of each act of the drama of the village of Kamli before it was submerged in Lake Mangal Sagar. And then he opened his eyes which were slightly cocked, as though, like Alexander the Great he drew the wisdom of heaven with the left eye, which was tilted upwards, and from the earth with the right eye, which was tilted downwards. And he spoke:

'Like a child you are in your curiosity, brother. But if it will fill you with compassion for the human lot, I shall tell you this, my mythical story, and you can draw your own conclusions.

'Once upon a time, and it seems a long time ago, there stood at the bottom of the ravine there, now filled with the life-giving waters of Mangal Sagar, the selfsame village of Kamli, of which I have spoken.

'And though it was peopled by seventy souls, all told,

there were five men of this village, villains, if you would like to call them such, but men whose words counted for much with the ignorant, and who were able to persuade many to defy the light, for months, on behalf of the power of darkness.

'The chief of this group, who was moreover a landlord, owning some bighas of land, and headman of the village, was called Viroo. An old man of nearly eighty years, he sat upon the land, and upon his own life, like a leech upon a sick body, drinking away the blood without getting any fatter to the naked eye. He had a profligate son, called Prakash, a boy who stole jewellery from his mother's box and sold it in Ambala, but who was nevertheless much loved by his father and utterly spoilt by his mother, being plied with endless long tumblers of whey and copious portions of butter on his spinach and large loaves of maize bread. This Prakash beat up his own young sister, Yashoda, for stopping by the well a little longer than usual to listen to me reciting Hir in the distance, and he distinguished himself, during the events of those days, when his village was pitched in a battle against us, by rascally behaviour that has no parallel in the annals of the Punjab.

'The next in command of the forces of destruction was a goldsmith named Ram Jawaya, a dignitary with a tuft knot that protruded, always, beyond the confines of this small, greasy, black cap, the lashes of this eyes having been blown out by the smoke and fire from the hearth where he melted the jewellery pawned by the villagers, but whose greedy vision was still unaffected, so that he could see everything, evil in all that was good, whose mendacity had remained unabated in the fifty-five odd years of his existence on earth, during which his right hand never allowed his left hand to know how much land he was absorbing with his penman's jugglery, in the Jong account book where all the mortgages were recorded. His son, Dharam Dev, was not such a rouge as Prakash, the son of the landlord Viroo, but weak-chinned and pale-faced, this boy was a glib little talker, who constantly twirled his thin moustache in the belief that it was a thick one, though I am sure, he did this to give himself courage.

'And then there was the double-dealing, clever young man called Tarachand, who had gone to town and become a B.A. pass, though he had put in for the law and failed to become a vakil, in spite of the fact that he had sold his mother's land. Some said that he had turned sour because he could not get a job in the offices of the Sarkar, and that may have been the reason for his virulence. But to me he seemed the kind of man who could have sold his mother for his own good and set fire to the whole village if it had suited him, even as he surely lit the flames of the controversy which nearly ruined the fortunes of all the poor peasants. You know that our country is full of partial prophets, petty quacks posing as perfect Doctors, speakers of half truths promising total cures and before them we feel helpless...

'There were also two middle-peasants, brothers, named Jarnel Singh and Karnel Singh, who had served as Sepoys under the British Raj and retired with the rank of Havildar and Lance Naik respectively. They had failed to gain any wisdom from their wanderings across the earth and never forgot the two squares of land given to them by the Angrezi Sarkar in Lyallpur District, which they had to leave after the partition, even as many of us left everything we ourselves had, north of the Wagha Canal.

'A young boy named Bharat Ram, the son of the widow Siddhi, who had learnt to be a mechanic in a motor garage in Patiala town, stood aide from all these and seemed to me, in his long silences, to be the superior of this nefarious gang of obstructionists, for he talked sense when he did dare to open his mouth before them and nearly swayed the villagers on the side of truth. And he it was who came with us, beating the drum, even as I went among the folk singing the songs, and shouting the words, which were to rescue the villagers from the mouth of the disaster that nearly befell them.

"Actually, how did the trouble arise and what happened?" I asked him impetuously in my eagerness to know how the crises had developed.

'Not so fast, brother, said Bali, the bard. As the poet Kabir has spoken: "What cooks slowly matures into a sweeter dish." And I shall tell you all if you be patient. You must understand, first, that part of the world today wants plenty for us black men and part of the world is opposed to this idea. While most men hesitate because they think two thoughts at the same time. And in the learned ones like you, many forces make for adverse ends....'

"Go, on, brother, go on," I said.

'Actually,' he continued, 'These people of Kamli did not know, at first, what was going on. They were the creatures of habit, whose chief god was *Dastur.* What was good enough for their forefathers was, they thought, good enough for them. And they did not know where they were going or what they really wanted. And though they followed their customs blindly, they suffered in secret. And then they were amazed that they were caught up in the web of suffering.

'And, yet, all the time they were fighting feuds with each other.

'Thus, landlord Viroo felt, that the whole of the village had been poisoned by the goldsmith Ram Jawaya, And goldsmith Ram Jawaya felt, that the cause of the downfall of the whole of the countryside was Babu Tarachand, B.A., who talked so much, mixing the words of Punjabi speech with Angrezi, and putting on kot-patloon to impress all and sundry, and ready to throw all the wise elders on the rubbish heap. The middle peasants, Jamel Singh and Karnel Singh, worked hard on the land and hardly had any time to think, but when they did manage to scratch their heads, they felt that the moment had come when both landlord Viroo and goldsmith Ram Jawaya should give up the headship of the village which these elders had enjoyed in rotation, and allow one of the younger ones among them to become the Chaudhri. And, all of these 'wise' ones, distrusted their sons, because the boys were seen in the company of mechanic Bharat Ram, the son of the widow Siddhi, who gave lifts to all his companions on his *phutt-phutti.*

'And thus the elders stood open-mouthed for the first few months, even as they stared at the glow of the giant lights, which shone during the nights to enable the labourers to keep vigil on the construction of the Mangal Dam. And they muttered curses against the Kali-Yug, during which the laws of nature were being upset by the wiping out of the distinction between day and night. And as they heard the *phutt-pphutti* of mechanic Bharat Ram making frequent trips to the site of the dam, three miles away, with one or two of the boys of the village holding on to him from the seat at the back, they were more furious with this mechanic than even with the builders of the dam. And when they realised that most of the villagers got better wages doing labour on the construction than they themselves had ever paid these men for work on their estates, they were filled with murderous rages...

'So they appointed the loquacious Babu Tarachand, B.A., top go and see the Tehsildar of the big village of Mangal and apprise him of the objections of the elders of Kamli against the upset caused by the demoniac construction... And Tarachand, they did not know, is a two-faced man, and his body is a mixture of many selfish attitudes. And with his own confusion, he can sow more confusion in each soul.

'Babu Tarachand, B. A., went proudly enough to meet the Tehsildar and came back thumping his chest at the victory he had secured.

The Sarkar is going to give us money by way of compensation for moving our houses in this village to a settlement near Chandigarh when Kamli is submerged in the artificial lake of Mangal Sagar that will fill the space between the two hills on our side, And I had secured the promise of the best lands in the basin, at the foot of the Himalayas, for us all...

"Compensation!" exclaimed Viroo

"For leaving our houses?" protested Ram Jawaya.

"A settlement near Chandigarh?" inquired Jamel Singh.

"You mean to say that you, son of an owl, have agreed on our behalf, that we will move out of our village...";

"Hallowed by the incarnation of the goddess herself!"

asseted old Viroo.

"If the land near Chandigarh it's anything like as good as the plots we had in Lyalljmr district," ventured Karnel Singh, "But what would this literate fool Tarachand know about the qualities of the soil!"

"Look, folks darkness has come," put in Ram Jawaya, "He has sold us all, as he would willingly sell his mother, for some advantage which the Tehsildar has promised him."

"Uncle," answered Tarachand, B.A. , "I have not sold you or the village, or myself, I am with you. And I think it is a crime that we should be moved to the barren deserts of Chandigarh, where dust storms blow from morning to night, and where no one is buying houses, even of the thickest walls, because nothing can keep away the dust! These engineers are trying to do our wheat farming in offices with typewriters. All theory and no go..."

"Then, learned one," said old Viroo, "sit down and forthwith write to the Sarkar to remove this construction, which is blasting away our hills and let us live in peace.

"To be sure," added Ram Jawaya.

"Han, han," confirmed Jarnel Singh and Karnel Singh.

'And though Babu Tarachand, B.A., had been tempted by the prospects of going to Chandigarh, where he might be able to bring influence to bear to secure a job in some office, after all, he sat down and did the bidding of the elders and wrote a petition to the Sarkar, protesting against the plan to submerge the village of Kamli in the artificial lake of Mangal Sagar.

'For sometime they all waited for the answer of the

Sarkar. As you know brother, at the best of times, our Sarkar bungles with the papers. Perhaps there are too many of those things, called files. But none of the clerks or officers of the Sarkar seem to take responsibility. They always pass on the applications, with their opinions, on to someone else, who might lose the papers, or may have too much to do to look at them. And so applications are seldom answered or forwarded higher up. So there was some delay in the arrival of an answer to the petition of the elders of Kamli from the Sarkar.

'And, in the meanwhile, as the construction of the dam proceeded, and the earthworks loomed as high as the nearby hills, Ram Jawaya, who had acquired twenty acres of land, in spite of the prohibition against mere money-lenders possessing the soil, went to pray to the goddess Kamli, one night accompanied by his wife, Dharmi. He put a silver rupee and a coconut before the shrine of red stone, and prayed that the goddess might make herself manifest and destroy the dam and save the village named after her. And though the goddess did not appear, Dharmi took it upon herself to go, at dead of night evading the big lamps, and did magic near the site of the constructions, by putting an earthen saucer lamp on the cross-roads with a little rice and sugar around it in the sign of the swastika. She breathed some secret prayers and returned home in the dark. This was the ceremonial of bygone ages masquerading as the worship of the Gods!

'The next morning the work on the construction proceeded exactly as it had done before the magic was done on the cross-road.

'Ram Jawaya, whom his wife had told of her magic, ground his teeth in bitterness at the frustration of his wife's design. As Dharmi had taken the wife of old Viroo, named Kala, into confidence, and Kala had told her husband Viroo, the old landlord swore foul abuse against the giant iron cranes, calling them the inventions of the devils!

'The middle peasants, lamel Singh and Karnel Singh, too, had been thinking of some direct action for ending the darn, which they knew would ultimately submerge their lands in the water and force them, a second time, to go and settle somewhere else.

'Sardar Karnel Singh said to Sardar lamel Singh: "Brother, I know of an acid, which can be put into a little bottle, which itself can be thrown on the head of the engineer, which will finish this evil construction"

'And though Sardar Jarnel Singh nodded his head affirmatively, he had grave doubts, whether the plan of his brother could end the mischief, which was more than the engineer at the darn. Still, he did not dissuade Karnel Singh from thinking what he had said.

'And Karnel Singh, being a man who believed in deeds rather than words, stole up one evening, to the house of the chief engineer, Sharma, while this worthy was having his food, completely unaware of his danger. The ex-sepoy threw the bottle of acid on the head of the engineer and ran away with his tail between his legs.

'The bottle did not burst and, fortunately, the engineer's face was saved from disfigurement.

'This incident led the police to make certain enquiries in the village of Kamli, and Sardar Karnel Singh was hand-cuffed and taken before the Magistrate, who put him out of touch with his companions by consigning him to the Ambala District Jail.

'There is an old saying in our country that a man may spoil another, just so far as it may serve his ends, but when he is spoiled by others he, despoiled, spoils yet again. So long as evil's fruit is not matured, the fool fancies: now is the hour, now is the chance.

'And so the elders, Viroo, Ram Jawaya, Jarnel Singh and Tarachand, B.A., sat in council and decided that the conviction of Karnel Singh must be avenged. They decided to ask all the villagers, who worked on the dam site to withdraw from work. And they exhorted their young sons, Prakash, the scion of the landlord; Dharam Dev, the offspring of Ram Jawaya; and Darshan Singh and Sudarshan Singh, sons of Karnel Singh, never to go with the mechanic Bharat Ram on his *phutt-phutti* which kept the whole village awake at night and which was itself a symbol of the evils of time.

'The peasants in the village, who had been earning good money with their labour on the dam, were in a quandary; if they stopped working on the construction they would lose the money, but if they did not heed the advice of the elders, the goddess Kamli might come and destroy them. So they went to mechanic Bharat Ram, who was foreman-in-charge of one of the cranes.

'I know why you have come,' said mechanic Bharat Ram. 'I have made my choice and will go on working here until the dam is complete. If you wish for the good life, then pay no heed to those oldies and carry on with your labour, put aside a little money, and breathe the air of new times. Otherwise, you can go back to work on the estate of Ram Jawaya, to whom you have already mortgaged your souls and your bodies..'

'Whereupon the labourers decided to continue their work on the dam.'

'The headman Viroo, the goldsmith Ram Jawaya, Sardar Jamel and Babu Tarachand, B.A., were highly incensed at this act of disobedience on the part of the serfs. They assembled before the image of Kamli and solemnly declared, in her name, that, henceforth, they would not share 'Hooka and water' with these rebellious village-folk.'

'About that time, came the order of the Sarkar that the petition of the elders of Kamli has been rejected and that all the villagers would get compensation immediately for being deprived of their houses, and that they would be given fertile lands to plough after the next harvest and before the water of the artificial lake of Mangal Sagar should begin to flow and submerge the village of Kamli.

'And the Sarkar was as good as its word. And there arrived the Tehsildar of Mangal to distribute one lakh of rupees to the villagers, the bulk of it going to the five elders and the rest to the small peasants.

'Never had the elders of this village, far less the small peasants, seen so much cash. Their eyes opened wide at the vision of the silver, and they put their thumb impression on to the papers and received the compensations — Seth Ram Jawaya and Babu Tarachand B.A., signing their names in the Hindi and Angrezi letters respectively.

'But do you think, when their tumbledown houses had been paid for they would give up the ill-feelings they harboured against the dam? To such men as these, the sight of greater harvests alone on other lands, might have vouchsafed some consolation. As they could not see the corn waving in the breeze before their eyes, near Chandigarh, they remained dead at heart.

'A few days after they had put the cash in their boxes, and secured these boxes with strong locks, they went to the temple of Kamli to thank her for the victory she had secured for them, and they begged her again for the boon, that the dam, which might deprive them of their lands, might be destroyed by her if only she would assume the from of a stroke of lightning.

'And then they waited for the miracle to happen.

'The sun shone. There were no clouds. So there was no lightning. And the work of the dam now proceeded faster than ever, because the Sarkar declared that the water must flow by the end of April.

'As the elders could not damage anything more than the track which led from the village of Kamli to Mangal with their footsteps, the younger folk began to intervene on their behalf.

'It seems that Prakash had asked to borrow the *phutt-Phutti* of mechanic Bharat Ram. Since the landlord's son had not learnt to ride the machine properly, mechanic Bharat Ram did not oblige. And this gave Prakash the necessary cue for action.

'Prakash proposed to the weak-chinned son of goldsmith Ram Jawaya, and to Darshan Singh and Sudarshan Singh, sons of Karnel Singh, that they should waylay mechanic Bharat Ram halfway from the village to the dam site, beat him up and deprive him of his *phutt-phutti.* Dharam Dev was not so eager to take part in this ambush, but Darshan Singh and Sudarshan Singh, whose father was still in jail for throwing the acid bottle on chief engineer, Sharma, were more than ready to revenge themselves on the mechanic, who surveyed the world from the top of the crane and was, in their opinion, now so stuck up that he hardly ever joined them in their pastime of poaching for the green mangoes in the villages around.

'The boys all went out, under the light of the stars, on the excuse of doing jungle-pani, and lay in waiting for mechanic Bharat Ram to go on to his early morning shift at Mangal. They heard the *phutt-phutti* starting off from the village and got into position behind the bushes, from where they could pounce on their victim.

'But as mechanic Bharat Ram came, tearing across the tract he sped past them long before they could rush out of the bushes. All that they could do was to shout abuse after him and eat the dust that the *phutt phutti* had started on.

'They went back to the village and decided to tell the labourers, who were due to go on their morning shift, that mechanic Bharat Ram has told them the day was a holiday at the dam site and no work would be done. It was certain that if the labourers did not go to work, their pay would be blocked, and then these people could be incited against mechanic Bharat Ram, on whose information the labourers would have stayed away.

In this plan, the boys succeeded. So solemnly did they talk to the labourers that the men believed it was a holiday and stayed away from the shifts.

'But, on the next day, they found that they had been

deceived and, knowing that their pay would be cut for absenting themselves, they asked mechanic Bharat Ram why he had spread a baseless rumour that there was a holiday on the previous day.

'Mechanic Bharat Ram was a man of few words and merely said that he did not know anything about such a rumour. And the labourers thought, from his parsimonious speech, that he had, indeed, bluffed them all.

'The vicious boys, and some of the elders of the village, played upon the suspicions of the labourers and roused them into a slow and simmering indignation against mechanic Bharat Ram. And, when, at the end of the month, their wages for one day were actually cut, the labourers were incited by Prakash to go and smash up the motor cycle of mechanic Bharat Ram, which stood under the shadow of the crane from the cabin on the top.

'The watchmen of the dam arrested the culprits, but mechanic Bharat Ram persuaded him to let them off.

'There are many kinds of people in the world, brother, but, mainly two types of characters, because there are two main ways of thinking and feeling: Some people look at everything only from the outside, and the others only from within. But, while most of the villagers were addicted to the crude lumps of experience, mechanic Bharat Ram saw all round fully and got the whole view. And he believed that the change in men's hearts was more important then the conversion of their heads from the negative gesture to the gesture of affirmation.

'Only, the inner change is hard to achieve. And not even his gesture in having the men released from the clutches of the police affected all those villagers easily. Instead, they only became more enraged, thinking that mechanic Bharat Ram was trying to be a magnanimous Lat Sahib, as the elders said.

'And, they persuaded the elders to cut him and his old mother, Siddhi, from 'hookah and water' from the village brotherhood.

'And the women folk of the village joined together and invoked the spirit of the goddess Kamli in the temple and declared, on behalf of the goddess, that old Siddhi would die.

'The giant machines on the Mangal Dam worked steadily, however, and it was announced that there were only ten days left before the space, on which the village of Kamli stood, would be filled up with waters of Mangal Sagar and the dam would begin to work.

'And; this time, not only the Tehsildar of Mangal, but the Head of the District, *Dipty* commissioner, also came, to persuade the villagers to quit their houses and go in the lorries which had been brought for this purpose, bag and baggage, to the new houses and lands that they had been allotted near Chandigarh. The *Dipty* Commissioner made a speech, using, for the first time in his life the Punjabi tongue, and though the villagers laughed out aloud at his accent, they were also somewhat moved by his appeal in the name of the Prime Minister. He said that they should allow the interest of the whole of India to prevail over their own and not cling to their plots in the hamlet of Kamli.

'But the sudden silence of the elders showed that they were not convinced. Only Sardar Jamel Singh said:

"If you be so concerned about our welfare, then why do

you hold my brother Karnel Singh in jail?"

'The head of the district answered immediately:

"If that be your only grievance, I shall order Karnel Singh to be released tomorrow and the remaining part of his sentence will be forgotten."

'And, thinking that he had played his trump card and that the villagers of Kamli had been won over, he returned to the rest-house of Mangal and sat down in his basket chair to drink his peg of whiskey in peace.

'On the next day, when Karnel Singh was set free, there was much rejoicing in the village, and everyone thought that now the elders would call the whole Panchayat together and persuade the villagers to leave in the lorries which were waiting under the banyan tree.

'But no such thing happened. Instead, the elders met and claimed the release of Karnel Singh as another victory for the village against the authorities secured for them by the grace of Kamli.

'At this juncture, the head of the district was seen to shake his head before the Tehsildar and chief engineer, Sharma, dolefully. And mechanic Bharat Ram, who they had asked over to advise them on the best way of achieving a change of heart in the villagers, sat dumbly with his head hung down.

'At last the *Dipty* Commissioner ordered his big motor to be got ready and declared that he would have to send many more policemen than were available in Mangal to round up the villagers of Kamli and transport them to Chandigarh by force.

'Whereupon mechanic Bharat Ram made so bold as to lift

his head and to say: "Sire when by returning evil for evil do we cancel the original evil and when do we not actually increase it? Ponder on Mahatma Gandhi's gospel of accepting suffering and cleansing oneself. And believe me that "There is only one man who can change the hearts of the villagers, and that man is Bali, the electrician, working in the powerhouse.'

'And how could Bali, the mechanic of the power house, succeed where the others had failed?" I asked.

At this Bali smiled, and then, averting his cockeyes, felt for a packet of Char Minar cigarettes from the pocket of his tunic. As the fluency of Bali's narrative ended in a quixotic smile, and he would not open his mouth beyond tasting the end of his cigarette, I was more than ever curious to know of the way in which he could have changed the village dead hearts into the attitude of life.

"Go on, then, brother, don't keep me guessing!

"The solution was simple," Bali said, after exhaling a large amount of smoke.

'I went up to the head of the district, who had asked me to attend on him the next morning. And I said to the *Dipty* commissioner Sahib:

"Preserver of the poor, perhaps I can perform the miracle...'

" 'I do not believe in miracles," said the head of the district.

"Forgive me, Sire, but I have chosen the wrong word. Give me a drum and let this boy mechanic come with me, and I think I can persuade the villagers of Kamli to move to

Chandigarh. You be from Delhi, Sire, and do not know that all India is yet a village, while you do the talk of the town. Our people need a different talk..."

'The Head of the District waved his head skeptically. And the Tehsildar was not more impressed than the *Dipty* Commissioner. Only, Sharma, chief engineer nodded and said:

" 'Acha, let us see what you can do. Take mechanic Bharat Ram with you and come back tomorrow with some good news or I will wring your neck for you."

"And you went and performed the miracle?" I said.

" 'To be sure, brother, no miracle did I perform. Only a trick and the job was done"

"But what trick? And how?..."

'Always in life, brother, when words have become meaningless, there is a need to discover a new impulse to solve any given problem. And this vital impulse has to be clothed in a new idea. And the new idea has to be put into a new combination of accents, and if these accents come deep from within the belly, which is the source of all movement and speech, then, perhaps, the words arise, in rhythm and song, and may move the listener. This is the truth behind all our poetry. And that is why all our saints and poets went, tambura in hand, singing the 'name' they had experienced in their hearts.

'And so I kept vigil that night and felt about in my belly for some new words which may utter themselves, like a cry from inside me.

'And, in the morning, I issued out towards the village,

with mechanic Bharat Ram on my side, a drum suspended like a garland round his neck. And while he beat the drum and woke up the villagers, I began to recite my new song.

"Ohe awake, awake, Ohe brothers, awake.

We have been crushed by our slavery to the idols.

Our homes are crumbling into dust and our roads are covered with thorns,

On every side is heard only the empty sound of trudging of our naked feet, and the muttered curses from our naked hearts..."

'And hearing the drum beats, and this wail of mine, the villagers crowded around me.

"The cock-eyed bastard, disturbing our sleep early at dawn!" muttered Prakash.

"The fifthy electrician Bali!" said Darshan Singh.

"The son of a pig!" said Sudarshan Singh.

"But, sons, he seems to speak the truth," said Karnel Singh.

"He certainly has a lilt in his voice!" said Jarnel Singh. "I have heard him sing Hir!" said Dharam Dev.

"Ohe, sing Hir to us".

'I did not sing the song of Hir, but repeated the words of my new song.

"Ohe we have heard that," said old Viroo.

"Now, proceed further and sing the song of God, early in

the morning, and make this village blessed, so that the evil construction there may disappear and our harvests flourish."

"Ohe, han, sing the auspicious song of Kamli, so that we may be blessed with riches!"

"Acha, I shall sing to the goddess," I said. 'But just remember the words of the Sage who said:

"Men build many chains thinking that they will be safe and secure, but the truth of the Gods breaks these small chains that bind men, by revealing the total vision. I am not the singer of a single tune, nor do I recite only one phrase. I sing of all, for the understanding of all, shrinking not from truth for fear of you all:

And I began to sing a song, on the spur of the moment: "Oh, divine bestower of food inexhaustible, be gracious upto us your blessings, Thou Shakti, who incarnated herself as Kamli in this village, and who has now incarnated herself as the power emanating from the giant dam of Mangal, give us food...'

"Sacrilege!" said old Viroo.

"Blasphemy!" said Ram Jawaya.

"The fellow is a liar!" said Babu Tarachand, B.A. 'But I sang my song:

"Oh, divine bestower of food inexhaustible, who incarnated herself as Kamli in this village and who is the saviour herself, in liquid form, at Mangal...

Mother, who is energy incarnated into the dam,

walking magnificently and slowly you will come,

and will release the electricity,

and new leaves will bloosom at your feet,

and mango groves will burst into shoot,

and flowers will have a wonderful scent,

and bees will hum and murmur,

and birds will burst into sound

and mild and fragrant breezes will come stirring the surface of the waters of canals,

and the stalks of corn will flutter,

and there will be enacted festivals on this blighted landscape and all hindrances will be removed.

and the tide of the waters of Mangal Sagar will wash away the stains...'

"Ohe! Bale! Bale!" chimed Jarnel Singh.

"He is cock-eyed, but seems to have a good voice!" said Ram Jawaya.

'A poet and don't know it' said Babu Tarachand, B.A.

"Ohe, boys, sing with me in chorus, to the tune of mechanic Bharat Ram's dholak. Join the stream of the song. For thus are sins cured through the meeting of heart and heart, and thus do the subsidiary streams of doubt fade and mingle in the main-stream of life-giving waters:

"Oh, divine bestower of food inexhaustible,

Be gracious unto us and give us your blessings, Thou Shakti who incarnated herself as Kamli in this village,

And who has now incarnated herself as the power emanating from the giant dam of Mangal..."

'And lo and behold! the boys sang with me in chorus.

'And, then the village folk and the elders joined in slow, embarrassed accents, and they forgot themselves, as the drum beat up the rhythm of the song.

'And as they accepted the tune of my lilt, they also accepted the words.

'And they followed me to the head of the district and agreed to move to Chandigarh. For, they really believed that the goddess who had incarnated herself in their village, as Kamli, had now re-incarnated herself as electricity in the new dam.'

13

The Tractor and the Corn Goddess*

My Uncle Chajju it was he who really caused most of the trouble about the tractor. Of course, not being a devout person he was not the person who raised the slogans 'Religion in Danger,' 'The invention of the Devil,' and so forth. In fact, as soon as the affair began to assume the form of a Hindu-Muslim issue, he literally put his foot down on the machine and very proudly had himself photographed, as a Sahib has himself photographed with his foot upon the back of a tiger which a Shikari has actually shot. Nevertheless, it was a phrase of his which was responsible for the whole rumpus, or rather a great deal of it.

The facts of the case, which has assumed the significance of a legendary happening in our parts, were these. When the big landlord of our village, the Nawab Sahib of Bhagira; died, his only son, Nawabzada Mumtaz Ali Khan, who was reputed to be a worthless, irresponsible fool, addicted to much European habits as bad company and drink, came home from

---

* From *The Tractor and the Com Goddess and Other Stories.*

abroad and started to behave in a manner which most people thought was quite mad, or to say the least, somewhat strange. For, in the old days when a Zamindar died, his son and heir generally levied a tax for the funeral expenses on the peasants and followed it up by levying another tax still for the motors and the horses he had brought and generally made the peasants aware of the advent of a new order. But, on his arrival, Nawabzada Mumtaz Ali Khan issued a proclamation that the sum *of* seven lakhs, which has accrued through the illegal dues of the previous year would be distributed equally to all the peasants of his seven villages and that anyone who came to see him and put token money at his feet before making his plea, would not be listened to at all, and that uncle Chajju, who was the ring leader of the goondas of our parts and had been exiled was to be allowed to come back.

Most of the peasants, whose fathers, grandfathers and great grandfathers had been known to pay Nazrana, though secretly happy at being relieved of illegal exactions, still thought that it was bad form on the part of the new Nawab and a breach of the old custom, for, they said: 'After all the Zamindar is in the position of a ma-bap to us.' And uncle Chajju came back thumping his chest like Goonga, the famous wrestler, the Rustum of Hind, and declared that the new landlord was simply yellow and frightened of him. .'

When Mumtaz announced his next set of reforms, that he intended, by deed poll, to renounce all rights to his land and formed a Co-op in which all the tenants had equal shares, there came various deputations from the elders of the villages, relations and friends to restrain him from his insanity before the papers finally went through. The Deputy Commissioner of the area called the errant boy to him and reprimanded him severely for betraying the trust reposed in him by his forefathers, the community and the Sarkar. And, needless to say, the papers were annulled and the reforms were not executed.

Of course, Mumtaz was nothing if he was not a stubborn mule, once he had got hold of a notion in his head. And he began a long series of debates with the Sarkar about his right to divest himself of the land and yet avoid a Court of Wards being imposed on him. But while this matter was still dragging on and all kinds of opinions, good and bad, were being expressed by people about the Nawab's strange behaviour, he brought in that tractor which caused the biggest crisis of all.

Certainly Mumtaz had chosen the wrong moment to introduce this gadget on his estate. For, the months of talk about the new-fangled ideas which he had brought from Europe, and adverse comments on the long-haired, unkempt, dishevelled men and women, called, 'Comrades,' who went in and out of the 'Big house,' day and night, his reputation was in that state of stasis when one more error would lead to a final show down. Perhaps he forgot about the fate of Amir Amanullah of Afghanistan. Or, may be he modelled himself on Mustapha Kemal. At any rate, he only escaped by the skin of his teeth and he ought to be grateful that he is alive today.

The actual incident happened under the banyan tree just outside the big home one morning. The giant tractor had been fetched about eleven o'Clock from the Railway Station by Comrade Abdul Hamid the Engineer. Abdul Hamid brought the monster engine not across the main road, which is mostly empty except for the Rabbi harvest and as the machine furrowed the earth deeply before it came to rest at Mumtaz's door, the peasants gathered from all sides, chashed the tractor, some shouting, some just staring, some whispering to each other, all aghast with wonder or fear at this new monstrosity which had appeared in their lives and which threatened to do something to them, they knew not what.

It was at that juncture that uncle Chajju took the lead in the crisis. By one expletive he crystallised the feelings of all of them.

'Rape-mother,' he said caustically, even as he sat smoking the hubble-bubble under the banyan tree.

'That's right,' old Phagu chimed in. 'I hear it tore up the earth as it came along.'

'The earth then has been desecrated!' said Shambhu Nath, the Brahmin priest.

'*Han,* the Corn Goddess, the mother, the giver of all food, has been raped!' said his devotee Dhunni Bhagat, running up behind him.

'*Toba! Toba!*' said the Maulvi of the mosque, rolling his eyeballs and touching his ears under his green turban.

'Rape-mother!' repeated uncle Chajju. 'Why doesn't this boy Mumtaz come out and tell us what is in his mind, the secretive one. What is his game?' and he wore a quizzical expression on his frank face, which was more the index of a hurt pride than anything else, almost as though being an open-minded, hearty, old rogue he resented the fact that Mumtaz had not taken him into his confidence.

'I hear,' said Jodha, the oldest peasant of the village, 'that as the White race has never possessed the Shiva-Shakti which was in the sinews of our people, they have been inventing all kind of artificial medicines to make themselves potent. If it is true, what Dhunni Bhagat says, that the Corn Goddess has been raped, then this instrument ought to be sent back across the seas to the perverts who have invented it... Why, our religion, our shame is involved! Darkness has descended over the earth. What are things coming to? That our boys should be supposed to be so weak that they can't plough the land with the good old wooden plough! That I should have lived to see this insult to our race!'

'*Ohe chup kar,* Baba! said Chajju. 'It is not your voice we want to hear, but that of this young landlord of ours.'

'*Toba! Toba!* whispered the Maulvi rolling his eyes and touching his ears.

'Why are you touching your ears and whispering because we have spoken the truth!' said devotee Dhunni Bhagat. 'You are very shocked at our language but seem not to care that our mother earth, the Corn Goddess, has been desecrated...'

'To be sure, it is a question of religion,' said Shambu Nath. 'No Hindu landlord would have brought an artificial instrument like this to tear up the earth of a Mohammedan village.'

'To be sure! said Tirath, a crotchety, old shopkeeper, 'our religion has been despoiled.'

'*Ohe chup,* stop this kind of foolish talk and call that young son of a gun to come and explain to us what he has inflicted on us,' counselled uncle Chajju.

'To be sure! To be sure!' said one of the young peasants.

'It is probably an electric machine, with power stored in its belly,' said another.

'Uncle Chajju is right — we must know what it is for?' opined yet another and tried to touch the tractor ever so gingerly.

'Ohe careful, Ohe careful, it is the magic of Shiva-Shakti in a new form,' speculated Jodha. 'The invention of the Ferungis, who have weakened our race. You might die of the touch as the crows on the electric wire die every day.'

'Our Mahatma had already warned us against such machines,' said Dhunni Bhagat. 'We will not stand for the rape of the Corn Goddess, specially under Congress Raj.'

At that instant Abdul Hamid, the Engineer, emerged from the big house.

'Now then, come and tell us your meaning in bringing this here,' challenged uncle Chajju.

'Get away, get away, don't crowd round the Tractor,' said Hamid arrogantly, 'Nawab Sahib is coming.'

'Ohe look, folks, our religion has been despoiled!' shouted Dhunni. And he talks like this, Our Corn Goddess...'

'Yes, there is leather on it, I am sure, somewhere,' added Shambu.

'Go, go, lentil eaters,' shouted Hamid.

'Don't you insult the priest of the Goddess after you have trampled upon her body!' said Dhunni.

'Don't you bark,' said Hamid, measuring himself up against the devotee. with his torso stretched tight.

'*Toba*,! *Toba*! sighed the Maulvi and wagged his beard,

'Come, Come, boys,' counselled uncle Chajju. 'There is no talk of religion or the Corn Goddess or anything like that. All we want to know is what is this machine, how it is going to be used and what it is made of...'

'To be sure, to be sure, uncle Chajju is right, that is what we want,' said the boys of the village.

'I can settle that easily,' said the Nawab craning his head behind the knot of men who had gathered round Hamid, the Engineer. 'It is a Tractor — that is what it is called.'

'So it is the rape-mother tractor!' said Chajju partially satisfied.

'It has despoiled the body of our mother, the Corn Goddess!' shouted Dhunni.

'It has ruined our religion,' said Shambu.

'We will have no truck with this Tractor,' said Jodha. '*Toba*, *Toba*!' said the Maulvi.

'Ohe, stop this loose talk, said uncle Chajju. 'Let him explain now, let him talk since he has broken his vow of silence, the shy boy.'

'Well, it is a machine which can do the work of a hundred bullocks in one hour. It will till the land of all our seven villages in a fraction of the time that it now takes us to plough it.'

'Are you sure it is not a *gari* with hidden guns in it?' asked Chajju. 'You haven't brought it to shoot us down with, have you?'

'There is probably imprisoned here all the Shiva-Shakti

which the white race has robbed us of during their rule here,' said old Jodha.

'There is magic power in it!' said Phagu.

'Jinns,' said another peasant.

Bhutts?' said yet another.

'Don't be so suspicious, brothers,' said the Nawab, 'It is for your good that I have brought it. It is only iron and steel, so tempered as to plough the land quickly.'

'I would like it to be taken to pieces before I can believe that there is no magic in it,' said Phagu. 'And Jinns and *Bhutts* ?'

'Ohe it is the Shiva-Shakti, fools,' assured Jodha.

'It is all right so long as there is not a gun concealed in it,' said Chajju. 'That is all I am concerned with, for I am a man of peace!'

At that there was loud laughter, for my uncle Chajju is too well known as a cantankerous, quarrelsome creature to be altogether accepted at his own valuation as a man of peace.

'Well,' said the landlord after the amusement had subsided, but before the atmosphere of goodwill built up at the expenses of Chajju had altogether evaporated, 'The Tractor is yours and you can take it to the fields.'

'I suspect it is like the decoy wooden horse that was used by the soldiers in the story of the land across the seas!' said Phagu shaking his head sceptically.

'I think, Baba!' said uncle Chajju. 'You are right in suspecting this engine. And I agree with you when you ask for it to be taken to pieces before our eyes. We will only be content if it is reassembled before our own eyes. Because, then, we can learn to master all the Jinns and *Bhutts* in it!'

'Uncle Chajju,' said the landlord, 'I can see your meaning. It is right that you should be able to contact the Jinns and *Bhutts* in it. I nominate you to be the foreman under whose supervision the Engineer Sahib will take it to pieces. And then you shall learn to drive it, so that all the demons in it do the rough work of the village and give us more time to sleep under the shade of this banyan in the afternoons.'

'It is a great shock to my sensibility to learn to harness a steel plough,' said uncle Chajju, 'especially as I have never got over my love for my two bullocks who died in the drought, but I don't mind putting myself out a little if all of us can really have a longer siesta... In the hot weather there is no place like the shade of this banyan.'

Uncle Chajju is one of those funny men who has only to open his mouth to say a word to make people laugh. Perhaps it is his manner more than his method. Certainly, it is the tonal quality of his *theta* Punjabi accent that gets the villagers like a contagion. The amusement created by his speech reconciled all the recalcitrants to the Tractor, though not until after it had really been pulled to pieces and each peasant had touched it several bolts and knobs and felt the motive power of its dynamo next to their ears. After the terror of Jinns and *Bhutts* had been appeased and curiosity satisfied, it remained for honor to have its due share. The Nawab photographed all the villagers with the Tractor in their midst. And, of course, uncle Chajju, in the role of the new driver, stood like a colossus right in the foreground of the picture, as a Sahib stands with his foot upon the back of a tiger which a shikari has actually shot.

14

A Kashmir Idyll*

It was about ten years ago, during a brief visit to Kashmir, that the incident I am going to relate took place. But neither time nor space has blurred the deep impression it made on me then, and it has haunted me for many days, so that I must needs put it down.

There were originally four of us in the party including myself, the three others being a tall, imposing Sikh gentleman, both tailor-made and God-made; a sensitive young poet, a Kashmiri whose family had emigrated to the plains and made good as Kashmiris always do when once they have left the land where, though nature is kind and generous, man has for centuries most foully and cruelly oppressed man; and a hill boy who cooked for us.

We had loaded our luggage on a tonga and walked the three hundred and seventy-five miles on the road from Jammu across the Himalayas in slow stages, by the beds of the silent Ravi and the surging Chenab. On the peak of the Banihal we had held conversation with the wind that comes from the Kashmir valley, bearing a load of loveliness and pain, the

* 'From *The Barber* s *Trade Uion and Other Stories.*

golden exhalation of the saffron and the white sights of a people who toil unrewarded.

We had descended to the natural spring of Ver Nag from which a few drops of water trickle into a stream that becomes the River Jhelum at Islamabad, where it divides the whole valley into two halves and flows into Lake Wullar and then cuts its way through two hundred miles of mountains into the plains.

From Ver Nag, a village of dark and labyrinthine streets full of small mud huts, the multicoloured flowers on whose roofs give no hint of the misery which dwells within, we had traversed the main valley by a dusty road bordered by cubist poplars and cypresses.

We had made our headquarters in a houseboat at Srinagar. Then, taking the advice of a tourist's guide book which the government of His Highness the Maharaja of Kashmir had designed specifically for the use of English visitors, though a few Indians also took advantage of it if they had a smattering of the wonderful, official language, we had decided to undertake short trips to the remote valleys and the unspoiled outlying ranges of the Himalayas within the borders of Kashmir.

We visited the Sonamarg valley where the scarlet eyes of the morning are blinded by the glare of the snow that lies perpetually on the mountain peaks, leading through the Zogila Pass to Chotta Tibet, and where the sleep of the night is continually disturbed by the growling of the angry Indus rushing through glaciers and across high rocks and boulders on its tortuous passage across the Punjab.

We pushed by a difficult track across a crumbling mountain to the cave of Amaranth, where the dripping of water from melting crystals form a snow image of the shape of a phallus, which the superstitious go to worship in thousands at a particular time of the year, believing it to be the penis of the Great God Shiva.

We went to Gulmarg, the valley of wild roses; to Lilanmarg, where the lilies of the field grow for miles and miles, angelic and melancholy. We ascended to Aparwat, the high peak above Gulmarg, on top of which is a crystal-clear pool that echoes back the faintest whisper.

We saw Gangarbal and Hari Parbat, the Shalimar and the Nishat; we went everywhere, devouring the beauty of Kashmir's landscapes, trudging along its byways, loitering among its stars, squandering whole days and weeks in search of exquisite moments.

And then there was nothing left to do except to sail among the waterways of the valley, to seek new harbours for our houseboat in the Dal lake and in the shadow of the various gardens, wherever the caprice of our idle wills directed the heart-shaped oars of our boatmen.

A cousin of the poet of our company, a nobleman and courtier of His Highness the Maharaja, who had sought us out in an obscure corner of the Dal, and showered the blessings of fruit and meat and drink upon us with a generosity that betokened his eminence and his affluence, offered us the hospitality of an island he possessed near by.

Though greatful for his kindness, we had been finding the gentleman's hospitality rather embarrassing, because it involved us in a friendship with the great man which we could not spontaneously accept. For His Grace was rather a silly young man with the manners of a lout and a high blood pressure in his too opulent flesh, so we excused ourselves by saying that we were intending soon to complete our tour of the valley by going in our kitchenboat to the Wullar. But it was not so easy for us to escape from the tentacles that he spread around us by that slick and sure turn of phrase that had so obviously carried him to his high position at Court. He suggested that if we didn't accept his hospitality he would like to accept our hospitality and accompany us to the Wullar 'In your kitchenboat for a change, because,' he said, 'I am tired of this grand style in which I have to live, and would like to be one of you.'

We were so bounden to the Nawab Zaffar Ullah, as the worthy was called, for the many favours he had heaped on us that we naturally could not refuse him, even though he became more patronizing and added that not only would he like to come with us, but two of his most intimate friends would like to accompany us also, and that he would like to supply provisions and order extra boatman for our service on the way.

We were in for it, and we accepted all his offers because it would have been more strenuous to find excuses than to let ourselves become completely ineffectual pawns in his high hands. And accompanied by him and his friends (a surely little judge of the High Court of Kashmir, and a most superficial young trader in hides and skins), we started one evening.

The shades of night were falling and we floated through the heaven and the earth in a dream as yet slightly disturbed by the Nawab and his companions.

The river flowed, and our boat flowed with it, without much help from our boatman, his wife, his sister, or his little daughter.

But we had hardly retired to the silent places of our heart when dinner was announced.

The Nawab had brought a sumptuous meal prepared by this servants all ready to be served — rice coloured and scented with saffron curried fowls perfumed with musk, and there were goblets of champagne, bottled in 1889.

Having compromised us into accepting his delicious food, it was only natural that the Nawab should deem it fit to amuse us with the gifts of his speech. He told a few dirty stories and then launched into a discourse of which the ribaldry was so highly spiced with a deliberate obscenity that whoever felt nauseated or not, I, at least, who have never been overrighteous, turned aside, thought of the pride of my emotions, made my words the stars and surrendered myself to the bosom of the night.

When we awoke at dawn, our boat had unbarred the floodgates and glided into a veritable ocean of light. For, as far as I could see, for miles and miles, the azure waters of the Wuller spread around us, fluttering a vast expanse mercury within the borders of the fiery sun-scorched hills.

The Nawab sought to entertain us with a song. But his voice was cracked and only his two friends sat appreciatively acclaiming his genius, while we wandered off to different points of the boat, helping with the cooking, dressing or lazily contemplating the wizardry by which nature had written a poem of broken glass, crumbling earth and blue-red fire.

'For, truly, the Wullar is a magnificent spectacle under the red sky at morning.

I gazed upon the placid plain of water spellbound, enchanted. I lent myself to the whispers of the rippling breeze that was awakening the sleepy lotuses: tempted by an unbearable desire to be one with it, I plunged headlong into its midst and bathed in it to my heart's desire. Then I sat, sedulously noticing the blandishments of the elements from the shadow of a company under which the Nawab and his friends played cut-throat bridge.

By ten o'clock we had crossed the lake to Bandipur, a dull, insignificant little village on the take to Gilgit, the last stronghold of British Indian power before the earth ventures out into the deserts of Central Asia, uncharted except by shepherds till the Soviets brought steel plough of prosperity there.

The Nawab here ordered the Tehsildar to bring him tea, chickens, five dozen eggs and some fruit for our delectation. And he took us about to the dirty houses of the village to show us off, or rather to show himself off, to the poor inhabitants of the township.

Our boatman came running and said that we should hurry because he wanted to row us across the middle of the lake before noon, as a squall generally arose in the Wullar every day at noon, and it was likely to upset the boat if the vessel hadn't already crossed the danger zone before midday.

The Nawab abused him in Kashmiri, a language in which curses seem more potent than prayers.

We pressed the boatman's point, and since. His Grace could not swear at us, he said he would get a man on *begar* (forced labour) to help the boatman and his family to row across the lake more quickly, and he tarried.

The boatman came again after half an hour and found us all waiting impatiently for the Nawab's return from a visit to the lavatory: His Grace had suddenly thought it fit to have a hair cut and a Turkish bath in a *hamam,* and he didn't care what happened to us. When he did merge from his ablutions, and heard not only the insistent appeals of the boatman, but our urgent recommendations, he, as a mark of his favour, clemency, or whatever you may call it, forthwith stopped a young man of the village who was walking along the cobbled high street and ordered him to proceed to our boat and help to row it to Srinagar.

'But Srinagar is fifty miles away, Sire', said the young man, 'And my mother has died, I am on the way to attend her funeral.'

'Swine, dare you refuse?' snarled the Nawab. 'You are a liar!'

'No, Nawab Sahib said the man, joining his hands. 'You are like God in mercy and goodness. Please forgive me. I am footsore and weary after a twenty mile march in the mountains where I went to fetch my uncle's donkey. And now my mother has died and I must see the Mullah about securing a place for her burial.'

'Run, run towards the boat', bawled the Nawab, or, I'll have you flogged by the Thanedar. Do you not know that this is the kingdom of which I am a nobleman? And you can't refuse to do *begar.*'

'But Sarkar...' murmured the young Kashmiri, his lips

trembling with the burden of a protest which could not deliver itself in the Nawab's face, which glistened not only with the aura of light that the barbar's massage had produced but with the anger which the man's disobedience has called forth.

'Go, to the boat, son of an ass', shouted the Nawab and raised his hand.

At the mere suggestion of the Nawab's threat to strike, the young man began to cry, a cry which seemed childish and ridiculous in so grown-up a person, particularly because there were no tears in his large, brown, wide-awake eyes. And he moaned: 'Oh, my mother! Oh, my mother', mechanically, in a voice which seemed to express more the cowardice of the Kashmiri which has been bred by the oppression of one brutal conqueror after another, than his very own real hurt.

But the Nawab was too thick-skinned to see the hurt in the man's soul. He looked at the big eyes weeping without tears. and heard the shrill crescendo of his cry, and began to laugh.

'Let us leave him, Nawab Sahib', we said, "We will give the boatman a hand and row across the lake to safety if we hurry.'

'Wait, wait', the Nawab said', as he caught hold of the man by his left ear and, laughing, dragged him towards the boat.

The *begari,* who had begun to cry at the mere suggestion of a threat, howled the heavens down at the actual impact of the Nawab's hand on his body, while the Nawab, who had only laughed derisively at first, now chuckled with a hoarse laughter which flushed his cheeks.

The man extricated his ear from the Nawab's grasp as we were about five yards from the boat, and, perhaps because he thought he had annoyed His Grace by so overt an act of disobedience, he knelt down at his feet and, still sweeping and moaning, joined his hands and began to draw lines on the earth with his nose as a sort of penance for his sin.

At this the Nawab burst into redoubled laughter, so that his face, his body itself, seemed to swell to gigantic proportions and tower above us all.

'Look!' he said, flourishing his hands histrionically without interrupting his laughter.

But the situation which had been tense enough before had become very awkward now as the man grovelled in the dust and rolled about, weeping, walling, whining and moaning and sobbing hysterically with the most abject humility.

'Don't you weep, don't you moan, fool!' said the Nawab, screwing his eyes which were full of the tears of laughter, and he turned to the boatman, saying: 'Lift the clown there and put him on the boat.'

The boatman obeyed the commands of the Nawab, and His Grace having stepped up to the deck behind the *begari,* we solemnly boarded the vessel.

The *begari* has now presumably half decided to do the work, as, crying his hollow cry and moaning his weird moan, he spat on his hands and took up the oar.

The Nawab, who cast the shadow of his menacing presence on the man, was more amused than ever, and he laughed hysterically, writhing and rumbling so that his two friends caught him in their grasp and laid him to rest under the canopy. He sought to shake them off with the weight of his belly and with the wide flourishing of his hands and the reverberating groans of his speech which came from his round red cheeks, muffled with continuous laughter.

The boat began to move, and as the heartshaped oars tore the water aside, the *begari* ceased to cry and grieve with the same suddenness with which he had begun.

'Look!' the Nawab bellowed, his hysterical laughing fit ending in a jerky cough which convulsed him as a spark of lighting shakes a cloud with thunder. 'Look!' he spluttered and pointed towards the *begari*.

But the balls of his eyes rolled suddenly; his face flushed ghastly red and livid; his throat, twisting like a hemp rope, gave vent to gasping, whistling noise, and his hand fell limp by his side.

We all rushed towards him.

One of his friends had put his hand on the Nawab's heart, another was stroking his back.

A soft gurgle reverberated from the Nawab's mouth. Then there was the echo of a groan and he fell dead. He had been choked by his fit of laughter.

The boat rolled on across the still waters of the Wullar the way it had come, and we sat in the terrible darkness of our minds, utterly silent, till the *begari* began to cry and moan again.

'Oh, my mother! Oh, my mother!'

15

The Price of Bananas*

During the informal pilgrimage of the ancient cities of India which I made last year, I came across many things, multifarious beautiful and squalid scenes, and a great deal happened to me, which I hope to record in the only language I know, the language of the sharpened pencil, the coloured crayons and the paint brush. But there was one incident which I remember that compels me to put pen to paper, because a mere drawing will not help. So I am venturing on a verbal description of this episode, which may, perhaps, prove to be as amusing as it is significant of certain shades of feeling in our vast country.

I was on my way from Faizabad Railway Station to Lucknow. As everyone knows, Faizabad is the name, given in the days of the Moghul Empire, to the ancient city of Ayodhya, the capital of Maharaj Dasaratha, father of the God-king Rama, the hero of the epic, *Ramayana.* But many people may not be quite aware of the fact that, after the time of Rama's just, righteous and brilliant victory over Ravana, the demon-king of Lanka, with the help of the monkey general Hanuman and his hordes of monkeys, lemurs, apes and

* From *The Power of Darkness and Other Stories.*

gorillas, the monkey army settled down in Ayodhaya under the shadow of protection of the hero Rama. And though, in time, many of the descendants of the God King Rama himself emigrated to different parts of the country, quite a few of the descendants have remained through the ages clinging to their heredity and preserving the traditions, the noble ideals, the rituals, and even the riotous excesses, of their ancestors.

In this respect, it may be observed that the Simians have preserved their glorious heritage, as well as their sense of hilarity, in a far more integral form than the humans. So that one can see thousands of monkeys, performing miracles, or tricks, just as you may prefer to call their antics, almost with the agility which General Hanuman brought to his noble task in helping Rama. Of course, as succeeding ages have brought more and more highly organised armies and improved weapons, the fighting skill of the monkeys has diminished through lack of regular training, until only the daring plans of the Pentagon for training gorillas and monkeys to fight in new wars, can revive their historic prowess. But the monkeys have lost none of their capacity for fun; and their instinctive ability to spot out a demon, whom they can fight or amuse themselves with, has remained as sharp and uncanny as of yore.

As I had arrived at Faizabad station, half an hour in advance of the time for the train's departure, I sat on a bench watching the Simian hordes frolicking on the trees and on the open platform. The monkey mothers were hugging their little ones tenderly as they descended now and then from their perches to collect half-sucked mango stones and the remainders of food from the platform. The older monkeys sat enjoying a good old scratch, which is so soothing in the hot weather, as they have obviously learnt from the loin-cloth wearing merchants of our cities. And the younger fraternity sat adroitly on the thinnest boughs of neem and tamarind, trees, camouflaged by the leaves and so poised as to jump down with alacrity in pursuit of any meagre spoils that may be visible in the famished landscape of Uttar Pradesh.

Just then the train was announced by the ringing of the station bell, and, like everyone else, my whole attention was concentrated on securing a porch for myself. I noticed that, in our evolution from the quadruped to the biped stage, we have not only grown much clumsier but also less chivalrous with each other.

The mad rush for seats in the third class compartment by men with heavy bundles on their heads was forgivable enough, but the struggle of the lower middle class for an unreserved seat in the intermediate class was degrading because of the loud words and gnashing teeth. Having qualified into the middle-class, through the expenditure of my savings on a Delhi show of my pictures, I got my reserved seat in the first class compartment easily enough, with the added advantage that this seat was by a window overlooking the platform. Some other passengers, two Sikhs and three bureaucratic looking brown Sahibs, in English suits, joined me in the compartment, and we all began to fan ourselves with whatever came to hand to dry the copious sweet which the rising heat of the summer morning brought to our bodies. I, for one, found the torrid atmosphere of the compartment unbearable and walked out on to the platform. The bureaucrats followed my example. And the shade of the two neem trees was heavenly. For a while, I watched the third class passengers, who were busy filling up their small earthen pitchers and beautiful syphons from the water pump. Then I was fascinated by the genius of a monkey in snatching away the loin cloth of a pious Hindu who had begun to take bath under the pump. The general amusement that was caused by this incident became hilarious laughter when, after the bather had supplicated to the monkey with joined hands, the generous Simian threw down the loin cloth from the neem tree at the man's feet. It seemed as though the Station Master had trained the monkeys to keep good order on the platform.

While all this was going on, I noticed that a gentlemen, a business man by the look of him, clad in a white muslin dhoti, a delicate 'Lucknow' tunic, and an embroidered cap on his head had come up towards our first class compartment and stood looking at the white reservation card to see if his name was on it. He recognised his name on the card, and turning beckoned to the coolie, who was following with his luggage, a big steel trunk and hold-all and several small baskets and a brass jug. Weighed down by the two enormous articles on his head, the coolie could not see the Seth. So the businessman shouted:

'Are, come here! Can't you see? Blind one!... Here!'

The coolie did not hear because he was still far away. So the Seth shouted again, lifting his hands as though in a panic:

'Are, here, hurry, the train might go!'

'Aya huzoor, aya...!' the coolie said as he quickened his pace.

But before these reassuring words could have reached the Seth, he was unnerved completely, not by any default of the coolie, but by the adroit skill of a monkey, who leapt down from the top of our compartment, snatched away the fine embroidered cap of the businessman, and got up to the neem tree.

'Are! Are! Father of fathers! What have you done, monkey, brother-in-law!'; the businessman shouted in utter confusion. And his face, which has been round and smug, was covered with perspiration.

By this time the coolie had arrived with his luggage and was waiting for orders. But the Seth had run up towards the tree over the pump and stood threatening the monkey with his fisticuffs and loud abuse. The more he abused the monkey, however, the remoter the monkey became. For, apparently, it was the same skilful Simian who had played the prank on the bather. And what added to the perplexity of the businessman was the completely unsympathetic attitude of the onlookers, who laughed out aloud or smiled as the Seth became more vociferous in his challenges, threats and imprecations.

'Look people,' he said stretching his hands to the crowd with a piteous and hopeless expression on his bespectacled face. He thought that the loss of his head-dress, which is the symbol of dignity in India, would be deplored by everyone and a sentiment of solidarity arise.

But the people just turned their faces away or looked stonefaced, as they often do for fear of being dragged into giving evidence before the police.

And the coolie made it worse by calling out,

'Sethji, where? Where shall I put the luggage?'

I told the coolie to put the luggage in the compartment, as I knew the Sethji had found a seat here. And I began to help him with the luggage.

As I turned from the compartment, I saw that a fruit hawker had come forward pushing his little cart and was telling the Seth that he would rescue his cap.

Sethji seemed to be only slightly relieved by the voluntary offer of the fruit vendor.

But the vendor went ahead, nevertheless, dangling a couple of bananas before the monkey with this right hand, and stretching out his left hand for the cap.

The monkey seemed to hesitate, not because he was not tempted, but because there were too many people laughing and talking and offering advice and he probably dreaded some punishment if he came down.

'Ao, ao, come down,' the vendor coaxed the monkey, lifting the bananas higher up, even as he walked up towards the bough on which the animal was sitting.

The monkey responded by climbing down cautiously to a branch which was almost contiguous to the stretched right arm of the fruit vendor.

The whole platform became silent, as the people, who had been laughing and making odd remarks, waited, with bated breath, for the impossible to happen.

—But the impossible did happen.

The vendor cooed in a soft voice and gestured to the accompaniment of *Ao, ao,* and the monkey, after looking this side and that accepted the bargain, taking over the bananas with his right hand while he released the wonderful embroidered cap, slightly crumpled with his left hand.

'Sabhash! What to say. May I be a sacrifice for you!' the different members of the crowd commented.

And the Sethji, to whom the cap belonged and whom the monkey had deprived of his dignity so suddenly rudely stretched out his hands towards the fruit vendor to receive the cap. His eyes were withdrawn as he had obviously felt very embarrassed at being made, by a cruel fate, the victim of what now seemed like the perverted sense of humour of the monkey; and he was eager to get into the compartment after the restoration, of his head gear.

The fruit-wallah came and humbly offered the Seth his cap, adding:

'Those *budmashes* are hungry. So they disturb the passengers. He really wanted the bananas..."

'Acha', said the Seth surlily and turned to go into the compartment.

'Sethji, please give me the two annas for the bananas which I had to offer to the monkey...'

'Are wahl What impudence! Two annas if you please! For what?... Sethji shouted each word, with the mingled bitterness of his humiliation at the hands of the monkey and disgust in the face of a grimy fruit vendor

'But Sethji?' protested the vendor.

'Han, han, Seth Sahib,' I added. 'Please give him two annas.'

'Han, han,' agreed one of the bureaucrats.

'Acha, here is your money, coolie. Four annas for you! And

an anna for you, fruit-wallah!' Sethji conceded.

'But huzoor!' the coolie wailed. 'Two big pieces of luggage and—'

'Go, go! Sala! Crook!' Sethji thundered, turning to the coolie. And he nearly came down from the eminent position he occupied in the doorway, to kick the coolie away.

The coolie went away but the fruit vendor persisted, saying:

'Sethji, be just, I saved your cap, the mark of your *izzat,* for you and—'

The businessman threw an anna towards him on the platform and went into the compartment.

The guard's whistle blew and everyone boarded the train.

The fruit vendor looked in from the window from outside to explore the compartment, so that he could make further please to the Seth. And, finding him settled down, by the Sikhs, he entreated with joined hands:

'Sethji, do not rob the poor! I tried to—'

'*Ja, ja!* Take rest! do your work!' the Sethji spat fire, while the frown on his face twisted his visage into an ugly, unhappy scowl.

'Give, him one anna more, Sethji.' I said with a straight face.

'You don't know, Sahib, you don't know these *budmashes!* They are in league. with the monkeys! Bananas are two a pice! Fancy asking for an anna for one rotten banana! '

This seemed to me outrageous and I was dumb with the shock of the astute businessman's calculations.

Meanwhile, the train had begun to move, and the fruit vendor first ran along with it, then got on to the footstep and clung to the window, appealing, threatening and pleading in turn. But Sethji had turned his head astray and was looking out of the window at the goods train on the other side.

At length the train passed the whole length of the platform and the frustrated fruit vendor dropped off after hurling the spiciest abuse on the merchant.

I looked at the bureaucrats, and the bureaucrats looked at me, while the Sikhs stared at the Seth, but the Seth kept his face averted from us and kept steadily looking out of the window.

When the train was well out of Faizabad station, he did sit back with his face, now towards the sanctum of the compartment, and began to see if his luggage was alright. Then he turned round to all of us and began to justify himself: "If he did not want to help me to get my cap back, he should not have offered the monkey the bananas! I did not ask him to help!..."

I could not bear this self-righteousness and, under cover of big words, tried to pontificate: '*Han, han,* all men are equipped with free will. They can go to hell or they can go to heaven... The rich *Sahukars* always go to heaven!...'

I impetuously tried to shame him by staring at him when I caught his eyes for a brief moment. But he was partly sheepish and partly knew me to be hostile. So he avoided looking in my direction.

The anger in my soul mounted even as the Seth seemed to cool down and assume an air of casual indifference. I felt that all the other passengers felt with the poor vendor and that the whole amusing occasion had ended in a sour and bitter sense of grievance against the businessman, who seemed tolerably well of from his clean clothes, but who had been so hard to the generous-hearted fruit vendor.

I took the only revenge I could take on this mean creature by drawing a caricature of him in the position in which I had seen him as he stood under the neem tree, supplicating to the monkey who had taken his cap away and I passed it on to the other passengers. The bureaucrats smiled, while the Sikhs began to laugh out aloud and were all for shaming the Seth by showing the cartoon to him. But I restrained them. I think he knew from the ease which arose after the cartoon had been passed round, that our relaxed smiles were the index of his discomfiture...

Part IV

THE COMIC VEIN

16

A Pair of Mustachios*

There are various kinds of mustachios worn in my country to make the boundaries between the various classes of people. Outsiders may think it stupid to lay down, or rather to raise, lines of demarcation of this kind, but we are notorious in the whole world for sticking to our queer old conventions, prides and prejudices, even as the Chinese or the Americans, or, for that matter, the English... And, at any rate, some people may think it easier and more convenient to wear permanent boundary-lines like mustachios, which only need a smear of grease to keep them bright and shiny, rather than to wear frock coats, striped trousers and top hats, which constantly need to be laundered and dry-cleaned, and the maintenance of which is already leading to the bankruptcy of the European ruling classes. With them clothes make the man, but to us mustachios make the man. So we prefer the various styles of mustachios to make the differences between the classes...

And very unique and poetical symbols they are too. For instance, there is the famous lion mustache, the fearsome upstanding symbol of that great order of resplendent Rajas,

---

* From *The Barber's Trade Union and Other Stories.*

Maharajas, Nabobs and English army generals who are so well known for their devotion to the King Emperor. Then there is the tiger mustache, the uncanny, several pointed mustache worn by the unbending, unchanging survivals from the ranks of the feudal gentry who have nothing left but the pride in their greatness and a few mementos of past glory, scrolls of honour, granted by the former Emperors, a few gold trinkets, heirlooms, and bits of land. Next there is the goat mustache — a rather unsure brand, worn by the *nouveau riche,* the new commercial bourgeoisie and the shopkeeper class somehow don't belong — an indifferent, thin little line of a mustache, worn so that its tips can be turned up or down as the occasion demands a show of power to some coolie or humility to a prosperous client. There is the Charlie Chaplin mustache worn by the lower middle class, by clerks and professional men, a kind of half-and-half affair, deliberately designed as a compromise between the traditional full mustache and' the cleanshaven *Curzon* cut of the Sahibs and the Barristers, because the Babus are not sure whether the Sahibs like them to keep mustachios at all. There is the sheep mustache of the coolies and the lower orders, the mouse mustache of the peasants, and so on.

In fact, there are endless styles of mustachios, all appropriate to the wearers and indicative of the various orders, as rigorously adhered to as if they had all been patented by the Government of India or sanctioned by special appointment with His Majesty the King or Her Majesty the Queen. And any poaching on the style of one class by members of another is interpreted by certain authorities as being indicative of the increasing jealousy with which each class is guarding its rights and privileges in regard to the mark of the mustachio.

Of course, the analysis of the expert is rather too abstract, and not all the murders can be traced to this cause, but certainly it is true that the preferences of the people in regard to their mustachios are causing a lot of trouble in our parts.

For instance, there was a rumpus in my own village the other day about a pair of mustachios.

It so happened that Seth Ramanand, the grocer and money-lender, who had been doing well out of the recent fall in the price of wheat by buying up whole crops cheap from the hard-pressed peasants and then selling grain at higher prices, took it into his head to twist the goat mustache, integral to his order and position in society, at the tips, so that it looked nearly like a tiger mustache.

Nobody seemed to mind very much, because most of the mouse-mustached peasants in our village are beholden of the banya, either because they owe him interest on a loan, or an instalment on a mortgage of jewellery or land. Besides, the Seth had been careful enough to twist his mustache so that it seemed nearly though not quite like a tiger mustache.

But there lives in the vicinity of our village, in an old, dilapidated Moghul style house, a Mussulman named Khan Azam Khan, who claims descent from an ancient Afghan family whose heads were noblemen and councillors in the Court of the Great Moghuls. Khan Azam Khan, a tall, middle-aged man is a handsome and dignified person, and he wears a tiger mustache and remains adorned with the faded remanants of a gold-brocaded waistcoat, though he hasn't even a patch of land left.

Some people, notably the landlord of our village and the moneylender, maliciously say that he is an impostor, and that all his talk about his blue blood is merely the bluff of a rascal. Others, like the priest of the temple, concede that his ancestors were certainly attached to the Court of the Great Moghuls, but as sweepers. The landlord, the money-lender and the priest are manifestly jealous of anyone's long ancestry, however, because they have all risen form nothing, and it is obvious from the stately ruins around Khan Azam Khan what grace was once his and his fore-fathers. Only Khan Azam Khan's pride is greatly in excess of his present possessions, and he is inordinately jealous of his old privileges and rather foolish and headstrong in safeguarding every sacred brick of his tottering house against vandalism.

Khan Azam Khan happened to go to the moneylender's shop to pawn his wife's gold nose-ring one morning and he noticed the upturning tendency of the hair on Ramanand's upper lip which made the banya's goat mustache look almost like his own tiger mustache.

'Since when have the lentil-eating shopkeepers become noblemen?' he asked surlily, even before he had shown the nose-ring to the banya.

'I don't know what you mean, Khan,' Ramanand answered.

'You know what I mean, seed of a donkey!' said the Khan. 'Look at the way you have turned the tips of your mustache upwards. It almost looks like my tiger mustache. Turn the tips down to the style proper to the goat that you are! Fancy the airs of the banyas nowadays!'

'Oh, Khan, don't get so excited,' said the money lender,

who was nothing if he was not amenable, having built up his business on the maxim that the customer is always right.

'I tell you, turn the tip of your mustache down if you value your life!' raged Khan Azam Khan.

'If that is all the trouble, here you are,' said Ramanand, brushing one end of his mustache with his oily hand so that it dropped like a dead fly. 'Come, show me the trinkets. How much do you want for them?'

Now that Khan Azam Khan's pride was appeased, he was like soft wax in the merchant's sure hand. His need, and the need of his family for food, was great, and he humbly accepted the value which the banya put on his wife's nose-ring.

But as he was departing, after negotiating his business, he noticed that though one end of the banya's mustache had come down at his behest, the other end was still up.

'A, strange trick you have played on me, you swine,' the Khan said.

'I have paid you the best value for your trinket, Khan, that any money-lender will pay in these parts,' the banya said, especially, in these days when the Sarkars of the whole world are threatening to go off the gold standard.'

'It has nothing to do with the trinket,' said Azam Khan, 'But one end of your mustache is still up like my tiger mustache though you have brought down the other 'O your proper goat's style. Bring that other end down also, so that there is no apeing by your mustache of mine.'

'Now, Khan,' said the banya, 'I humbled myself because you are doing business with me. You can't expect me to become a mere worm just because you have pawned a trinket with me. If you were pledging some more expensive jewellery. I might consider obliging you a little more. Anyhow, my humble milk-skimmer doesn't look a bit like your valiant tiger mustache.'

'Bring that tip down!' Khan Azam Khan roared, for the more he had looked at the banya's mustache the more the still upturned tip seemed to him like an effort at an initiation of his own.

'Now, be sensible, Khan,' the money-lender said waving his hand with an imperturbable calm.

'I tell you, turn that tip down or I shall wring your neck,' said the Khan.

'All right, the next time you come to do business with me I shall bring that tip down,' answered the money-lender cunningly.

'That is far, said Chaudri Chottu Ram, the landlord of the village, who was sitting under the tree opposite.

'To be sure! To be sure!' some peasants chimed in sheepishly.

Khan Azam Khan managed to control his murderous impulses and walked away. But he could not quell his pride, the pride of the generations of his ancestors who had worn the tiger mustache as a mark of their position. To see the symbol of his honur imitated by a banya — this was too much for him. He went home and fetched a necklace which had come down to his family through seven generations and, placing it before the banya, said:

'Now will you bring that tip of your-mustache down?' 'By all means, Khan' said the banya. 'But let us see about this necklace. How much do you want for it?'

'Any price will do, so long as you bring the tip of your mustache down,' answered Azam Khan.

After they had settled the business the moneylender said: 'Now Khan, I shall carry out your will.' And he ceremoniously brushed the upturned tip of his mustache down.

As Azam Khan was walking away, however, he noticed that the other tip of the banya's mustache had now gone up and stood dubiously like the upturned end of his own exalted tiger mustache. He turned on his feet and shouted:

'I shall kill you if you don't brush that mustache into the shape appropriate to your position as a lentil-eating banya!'

'Now, now, Khan, come to your senses. You know it is only the illusion of a tiger's mustache and nowhere like your brave and wonderful adornment,' said the greasy money-lender.

'I tell you I won't have you insulting the insignia of my order!' shouted Azam Khan. 'You bring that tip down!'

'I wouldn't do it, Khan, even if you pawned all the jewellery you possess to me,' said the money lender.

'I would rather I lost all my remaining worldly possessions, my pots and pans, my clothes, even my houses, then see the tip of your mustache turned up like that!' spluttered Azam Khan.

'Acha, if you care so little for all your goods and chattels you sell them to me and then I shall turn that tip of my mustache down,' said the moneylender. 'And, what is more, I shall keep it flat. Now, is that a bargain?'

'That seems fair enough,' said the landlord from under the trees where he was preparing for a siesta.

'But, what proof have I that you will keep your word?' said Azam Khan. 'You oily lentil-eaters, never keep your promises.'

'We shall draw up a deed, here and now,' said the money-lender. 'And we shall have it signed by the five elders of the village who are seated under that tree. What more do you want?'

'Now, there is no catch in that,' put in the land lord. 'I and four other elders will come to court as witnesses on your behalf if the banya doesn't keep his mustache to the goat style ever afterwards.'

'I shall excommunicate him from religion if he doesn't keep his word,' added the priest, who had arrived on the scene on hearing the hubbub.

'Acha,' agreed Azam Khan.

And he forthwith had a deed prepared by the petition writer of the village, who sat smoking his hubble-bubble under the tree. And this document, transferring all his household goods and chattels, was signed in the presence of the five elders of the village and sealed. And the money-lender forthwith brought both tips of his mustache down and kept them glued in the goat style appropriate to his order.

Only, as soon as Khan Azam Khan's back was turned he muttered, to the peasants seated near by: 'My father was a sultan.'

And they laughed to see the Khan give a special twist to his mustache, as he walked away maintaining the valiant uprightness of the symbol of his ancient and noble family, though he had become a pauper.

17

The Signature*

There is something sacred about a signature; it makes everything valid, puts the seal upon all undertakings, makes bonds real, guarantees securities, cements pacts of friendship and alliance between states, provides the ultimate proofs of integrity in the highest court of law. The signature is all in all. Even poets, when they publish new poems often call them 'New signatures'. And the radio uses a signature tune as its patent or hallmark. But especially do banks honour the signature; certainly they will not honour anything which does not bear a signature; to them the signature is almost omnipotent, omniscient, omnipresent, supreme!

Now, though everyone who draws a cheque knows the importance of the signature to the bank, through bitter experience of cheques coming back which the usual slip if they do not bear the signature, or if the signature is slightly wanky or blurred, there are still two kinds of peoples who have not yet realised the value of the signature. These are respectively some of the feudal gentry who live in 'Indian India' or the mofussil or on large estates in the country, and the very poor,

* From *Reflections on the Golden Bed and Other Stories.*

who have no bank account to their credit at all.

Of course, it may be said in extenuation of the last class of people, that the reason why they dishonour the signature is because they have been left illiterate. For they do make every attempt to come to scratch when a document is presented to them by putting their thumb forward for the blacking and imprint the very image of their soul, the mark of that stumpy, reliable finger on the page, thus honouring the unwritten convention that a mark of some kind is necessary in order to prove a person's integrity. But the conspicuous disregard of this convention by the former class of people, the feudal gentry, is rather surprising, to say least, and betokens an attitude which, though rather charming, causes serious difficulties, particularly to the business of banking — so the bankers say.

The banks, nowadays, are trying very hard to interest the feudal gentry to convert their gold into cash and let it flow, so that money should not remain buried in the earth in the classic tradition of our country and make a Midas of every grandee. But, as the nobility is incorrigibly lazy in appreciating the values of modernity there is a polite war going on between the nobility of the old world and the nobility of the new order.

Perhaps, one cannot call the tension that prevails between these brothers a polite war so much as a war of politeness, for there is no ill-will in this struggle or hatred or even contempt; there is only a certain impatience or irritation which is so often followed by laughter that it is more amusement than disdain.

One of the most amusing illustrations of this little war was provided the other day by the goings on between Nawab

Luqman Ali Khan Bahadur, nobleman and dignitary of Aliabad State, a Director of the India and Commonwealth Bank Ltd. and Mr. C. Subramaniam, Assistant Manager of this Bank.

The India and Commonwealth Bank Ltd. is a small but steady bank founded about ten years ago, which has, with the coming of freedom, been seeking to increase its business to contribute something to the making of the new India. In pursuance of this very laudable desire, they had recently promised a big loan on good interest to a new optical industry which was being set up by an enterprising young entrepreneur, against the most unquestionably sound guarantees. The papers were ready and had been duly signed by all the directors, save Nawab Luqman Ali Khan Bahadur. That was the situation and there was nothing very complicated or controversial about it. But Nawab Luqman Ali Khan, who had been sent the papers several weeks ago, had not just taken the trouble to sign them and return them. Meanwhile, the enterprising entrepreneur felt that the people of India were fast going blind for want of good eye-glasses, and the bank's normal business was held up.

The manager of the bank, Mr. Hormusji Pestonji Captain wrote many letters, reminding the Nawab Sahib Bahadur about his signature on the documents, but there was no reply.

As on all those occasions, when there is no answer to a letter, people begin to worry and postulate the most extraordinary fears and establish the strangest hypothesis, Mr. Captain began to think all kinds of things and got into a panic. The documents may have been looted on the way to Aliabad, he felt, for quite a few trains had been held up by armed gangs recently and ransacked; or the Nawab may have fallen a prey to a stray bullet in a riot; or he may have gone away to Pakistan. Anything was possible. And, as he waited day after day, the whole business became very nerve-wrecking. For the other directors might soon get to know that this loan was still pending and may feel he was inefficient.

So, after much worrying, he thought of a desperate stratagem: he would send the Assistant Manager, Mr. Subramaniam, to see Nawab Luqman Ali Khan at Aliabad and get his signature on all the documents. Subramaniam had won his way to assistant managership of the bank by dint of his command of figures, as well as his fingers, and certain sullen efficiency which, though not exactly American, was typical of the new Indian pioneers. Therefore Mr. Captain sent Mr. Subramaniam to Aliabad, not by rail, as that was not quick enough now after the Nawab's delays, but by air.

To the hard-working Subramaniam, who had, during twenty year's grind, got into a certain exact and unvaried relationship with the office-table and chair, this air trip was an extraordinary adventure and not altogether pleasant. For one thing, he was told by friends that it would be very cold in the air, and he went to the air-line office loaded with a hold — all full of blankets which made his luggage so heavy that he had to pay excess from his own pocket. Then, his digestion, trained on 'sambar' and 'rasam' revolted at the very first bite on the biscuits served by the air-hostess, and he felt, and looked, like a shrivelled up porcupine all the way. A further affliction was that at the midway station, where breakfast was served, he had to eat with implements other then those with which he had been used to eat in his orthodox life before. And, he made a fool of himself in the eyes of a couple of Indian dandies who were meticulous with their knives and forks and snobbishly contemptuous of those who were not so adroit. And, when at last he alighted from the bus at the airline office in the main street of Aliabad, he found himself in an incredibly native atmosphere where everyone was dressed in flowing India robes and he felt like a monkey in his badly tailored suit.

He tried to look for a taxi, but though some lovely Buicks glided by, there was no motor vehicle available for hire. Perforce, he had to jump on to a strange horse carriage called *ikka,* from which his legs dangled like the legs of a scare-crow which was being transported to the fields. And, all he could see being sold in the shops were colorful bangles and velvet shoes and 'Pan' 'Biri'. Subramaniam who had gone half-way to modernity thought that he had come to the backwoods and felt very depressed about it all, added to which was the usual panic at going to a strange place.

When he got to Zeenat Mahal, the palace of the Nawab Sahib Bahadur, he was further confused. For all the servants, sitting around the hubble bubble in the hall, gave him the once-over, cocked their eyes at each other and remained immobile. Apparently, they had been trained only to bow and scrape to the other noblemen of Aliabad, and a mere Madrasi, with pince-nez, arriving in an *ikka,* was not persona grata.

Mr. Subramaniam produced his card and asked to see the Nawab Luqman Ali Khan Sahib.

This time it was the servants and retainers who were confused, for no one had, within living memory, produced a white ticket of that kind with the request that it be transported to the Nawab Sahib.

The jemadar took it with gingerly fingers; and as Mr.

Subramaniam added a staccato phrase in Angrezi speech this dignitary ran towards the inner sanctums like a lame duck. Meanwhile, the other servants dispersed like wizened cocks fluttering away from the rubbish heap at the approach of a human being.

Mr. Subramaniam began to settle the *ikka* driver who unlike the Bombay *ghariwallahs,* immediately accepted what he was given, salaamed, and went off.

The jemadar emerged after protracted confabulations inside the sanctums of the palace and led Mr. Subramaniam towards a little guest house beyond the garden in the courtyard of the palace.

Mr. Subramaniam waited for a word of explanation which would provide the clue to what was happening to him, but the jemadar was silent, only being most polite and accommodating, bowing and salaaming now in a manner that seemed more than obsequious. And then he left Mr. Subramaniam with the words.

'Please rest and wait.'

Mr. Subramaniam took off his jacket and his shoes and lay back in the arm chair in the verandah. In a little while, a servant came and apprised him of the fact that the bath was ready. This made Mr. Subramaniam feel that things were moving after all. But, when he had finished his bath, changed into a new suit and come to rest in the arm the chair with a tea tray in front of him, and nothing happened again, except the passage of time on his wrist watch, he began to feel anxious. The laws of politeness in a Muhammadan household did not permit him to probe into any corner, even of the garden, lest there should be someone in purdah whose chastity might be outraged by the glance of a stranger's eye. The servants seemed to have disappeared. And Mr. Subramaniam's' hold on Hindustani speech was too precarious to permit him to shout and call the jemadar.

As the afternoon advanced towards the evening, Mr. Subramaniam's anxiety became a little more akin to irritation. And he began to pace up and down the verandah almost as though he was a prisoner of time. But this parade was not of much avail, and after he had walked to and fro for a quarter of an hour he sat down again and began to write a letter to the Nawab Sahib.

When he was half way through the letter, Nawab Luqman Ali Khan Sahib appeared, a jolly, rotund figure, dressed in a spotless white silk uchkin, tight trousers and a strange Aliabad-style round turban with no parting in front. And he was the very soul of affability, charm, grace and good humour. For he greeted Mr. Subramaniam almost as though the Assistant Manager was a long lost friend.

'I hope you had a nice journey. And, have my servants been looking after you?... Of course, you can't expect the comfort of such a modern city as Bombay in my humble abode... But we have a few modern places, you know. For instance, there is the Aliabad Club. I am just going there and you must come and meet my friends...'

'Sir, I would like to discuss those papers with you' Mr. Subramaniam interrupted. 'You see, Sir, I have specially come to get your signature...'

'Oh come, come, my dear fellow, you take work too

seriously. After all you have just arrived and you must see a bit of life. To be sure, we are not as advanced as you in Bombay, but... And we shall see about business matters tomorrow morning. After all it doesn't take long to put my signature on a paper... Come, don't worry. I want you particularly to meet Nawab Haider Ali, the Home Minister, and Nawab Wajid Mahumud, the Education Minister, and Prof. Ram Ratan Gupta — Mr. Gupta is our Finance Minister here. He is a wizard. He can count anything at a moment's notice. Come along now...' And he slapped Subramaniam's back with such cordiality that the poor South Indian nearly broke into two.

Soon, however, Mr. Subramaniam found himself seated in a beautiful Dodge and being dodged away across intricate bazars towards the cantonment and then through the magnificent portals of the Aliabad club into the monumental palace which housed this august institution.

But, while the drive was fairly diverting, because the Nawab Sahib kept up a running commentary on the wonders of Aliabad, Mr. Subramaniam's small soul, brought up on an occasional shivering visit to the CCI, shuddered with the fear of the unknown on his entry into the hall and shrank into nothingness in the face of the grandees who were assembled here in silk robes and golden turbans and velvet shoes. And, when he was introduced to the various dignitaries and they rose to shake hands with him, the forefingers of his right hand, with which he usually touched other people's hands, simply wilted like the falling petals of a dirty flower. One dignitary, Nawab Wajid Mahmud took it upon himself to instruct Mr. Subramaniam in the art of shaking hands:

'You know, my friend', this nobleman began, 'The

handshake is the symbol of affection and good-will. Let this love show itself with some warmth. When a person's hand clasps yours, give your full hand, with its real grip and not the four miserable fingers...'

This overwhelmed Mr. Subramaniam, until he blushed, flushed and began to perspire profusely. And, all he wanted was to be able to come to scratch, for there was no denying that this was life, brimming over, as it were, with warmth and hospitability. But his eyeglasses were blurred with the smoke of confusion and he was intensely relieved when he could sink back into a chair and contract into the littlest and most insignificant being on earth.

Nawab Luqman Ali Khan Sahib was much in demand. And for a while he went about meeting his friends. Meanwhile, the waiter who looked like a Nawab himself, brought a bottle of whiskey and some tumblers and began to pour out the liquor.

Soon Nawab Luqman Ali brought the Home Minister and the Finance Minister around.

Mr. Subramaniam had tasted whiskey twice or thrice and liked it, but his wife had smelt his breath and had given him a long lecture about how he was going to the dogs. Since then, he had found it easier to resist the temptation, but the persuasive tongue of the Nawab Sahib, his host, moved him, especially as the other noblemen added their 'Please' to his, in a most gracious Hindustani speech. And then the 'samosas' and 'Pakoras' arrived, with lashings of 'Podina' pickle, and the Southerner in Mr. Subramaniam felt the call of chillies and forgot all about his wife and Morarji Desai.

Soon he was happy, happier than he had been for years and those delicate negotiations for which he had been sent here, were obliterated by the fumes of alcohol and the seven-course dinner to which Nawab Wajib Mahumud, the Education Minister, insisted on taking the company in the club Dining Room after the appetisers.

Mr. Subramaniam slept soundly that night and was as good as dead to the world.

The next morning he felt the existence of a slight hangover.

When he had sufficiently recovered his sense it was about noon. He finished his previous day's letter to the Nawab Sahib and sent that in, requesting him to sign the documents.

There was no answer. Only the jemadar duly returned to the hall and sat smoking the hubble bubble.

And when Mr. Subramaniam made so bold as to inquire about the papers, the jemadar replied that the Nawab Sahib was still asleep, but that he was due to wake up soon, for there was to be a midday meal in honour of Mr. Subramaniam to which various friends of the Nawab Sahib were coming.

Mr. Subramaniam felt more frustrated than flattered on hearing the announcement. And then, there was the residue of guilt in his callow soul about his fall the previous evening. So he began to pace up and down the verandah of the guest house again and, fatigued by this useless occupation, he sat back in the armchair and tried to cultivate patience.

The warmth of the morning conduced to a light slumber and he only awoke when the jemadar shook him and told him the meal was ready and the guests had arrived.

If the dinner at the club had been a comparatively mild seven-course meal, the lunch at the Nawab Sahib's house was hospitality in the proper sense of that word, as it is understood in Aliabad. 'There were saffron tinted 'Pilaos' and rich 'Kormas,' tasty 'kababs' and fish, and fowl, cooked in the most luscious gravies. And even though Mr. Subramaniam took a little of everything, his stomach which was about the size of his fist or less, took in more than was good for him. And he found himself feeling drowsier and drowsier and could not even cope with the polite conversation about finance which Mr. Ram Ratan Gupta had started, far less bring the Nawab Sahib, his host, to talk of anything so concrete as those documents.

Nawab Luqman Ali Khan himself took the initiative to remind him during lunch that, after siesta that afternoon, he would bring out the papers to the guest house and go over them if Allah willed it so.

But Allah did not will it so. For though Mr. Subramaniam kept a vigil against all the seductions of sleep that afternoon, the Nawab was deep in slumber till the evening. And then he came like a whirlwind to ask Mr. Subramaniam to get dressed to go to the dinner to which Mr. Ram Ratan Gupta had graciously invited them. 'Don't worry about the papers,' he added, 'I have got them out and they are lying on my beside table to sign first thing tomorrow morning.'

So vociferously persuasive was the Nawab Sahib in imparting this information, that Mr. Subramaniam could not put a word in edgeways. And perforce, he went in and began to dress for dinner.

The dinner in Mr. Subramaniam's honour, given by Mr.

Gupta was as rich and sumptuous as the lunch given by Nawab Luqman Ali Khan; only, the number of vegetable dishes exceeded the meat dishes. But the general nature of hospitality was the same till Mr. Subramaniam began to recognise the unmistakable pattern of grace in Aliabad. There even followed the 'chain effect'; Nawab Haidar Ali even followed the 'chain effect'; Nawab Haider Ali suggested that it was his turn to invite Mr. Subramaniam now and that he would be happy if the honored guest, and the rest of the company, would come to the hunting lodge of his estate that very evening, for he had received a message from his shikaris, to say that a tiger had eaten the goat tied near the 'Machan' and was likely to repeat its visit. The laws of Aliabad hospitality demanded an acceptance of his noble suggestion and the company got into cars and was off into the depths of the night, illumined by a million stars.

The food and drink had broken the defences in Mr. Subramaniam's soul enough for him to lend himself to the seductions of this drive. Never before in his life had he tasted the delights of so novel an adventure as a tiger hunt. And, though he felt a slight hazard in this game, the fresh air, and the impact of the dense forests through which they were passing, made him forget everything and yield to a 'No care' attitude. As for those documents how could one think anything so obscene in the midst of this vast anonymity where nature seemed to cancel out all questions, especially banking?

And later the exhaustion of the tense wait for the tiger to appear, as they sat on top of the 'Machan' blotted out even his sense of individuality.

The tiger did not oblige the hunters by appearing. And,

after a' hearty breakfast, served in Nawab Haidar Ali's hunting lodge, the party of mankind had begun to resume its hold on work.

Mr. Subramaniam slept the clock round.'

And when he woke up, he suddenly found himself in a panic. It was strange how this confusion had come on him. But he sensed disaster. And, true to his prognostications, disaster it was that overtook him. For the Jemadar came and told him that the Nawab Sahib had been urgently called away to his estates in Madhopur and had left a message that Mr. Subramaniam Sahib was to wait till his return.

'But when will he return?' asked Subramaniam. 'Nawab Sahib did not say', answered the Jemadar. 'How long does he go for when he does go to his estate?' 'May be a month, may be a week, "huzoor".

Mr. Subramaniam let out an involuntary shriek of horror, which he later tried to disguise as the belchings of an overtaxed stomach. His whole body was warm with the heat of anger, resentment, fear and forced ingratitude.

'Go and fetch the papers from the Nawab's bedside table', he said to the jemadar.

The jemadar paused for a moment and looked askance at him.

Mr. Subramaniam understood. He took a ten rupee note from his pocket and gave it to the servant.

'Fetch the papers and get my luggage ready', he said.

'And hurry up for God's sake, hurry up!...'

The jemadar obeyed the commands of the honoured guest implicitly, What was more, he put the documents, Mr. Subramaniam, and the luggage, into the Ford which was waiting outside the hall and bade him a most respectful farewell.

Mr. Subramaniam took the night train back to Bombay, having to sleep on the floor of the second class carriage because he had not booked his birth in advance.

He was shivering with the ague of a terrible fear when he arrived at Victoria Terminus, the next morning, for he was sure that he would be sacked as soon as he appeared at the bank.

But Mr. Hormusji Pestonji Captain understood all as soon as the papers were put before him without the signature of the Nawab on them. He only asked Mr. Subramaniam, to look for the documents on which the first and only signature of Nawab Luqman Ali Khan appeared. And he had a rubber stamp made of this precious mark, impression or whatever you would like to call it. And he soon had the necessary papers ready to sanction the loan to the entrepreneur who had set his heart on preventing the people of India from going blind. And he cursed himself for not having thought of this simple expedient earlier.

'What is there so wonderful in a *sala* signature!' he said like an efficient Parsi..

Mr. Subramaniam lifted his eyes from the desk and signified agreement with a terrific forward movement of his abject little head and torso.

18

The Two Lady Rams*

When his Majesty the King Emperor (or whichever Government department it was that acted on His Majesty's behalf) conferred the title of knighthood on Lalla Jhinda Ram, in recognition of his sundry services to the British Empire, His Majesty's Government did not realise the awful domestic predicament into which they would put him. Of course, there is no way in which His Majesty the King Emperor, sitting seven thousand miles away from India, can ever get to know anything about the private lives of his subjects. And the department acting in his name which draws up the Birthday or New Year's Honours lists, though it is possessed of fairly well-documented confidential dossiers about the temperament, religious, political and social opinion of almost all notable persons as well as notorieties and particularly about the services rendered to the Sarkar by them, is singularly inept and formal about the human details of their lives. In the circumstances, the crisis which the honour of Knighthood precipitated in Lalla Jhinda Ram's house, was as inevitable as a sudden blow from Destiny, and brought more sorrow in its

* From *Tire 1ractor and tire Corn Goddess and Other Stories*

train than the joy which such a rise to eminence and respectability brings with it. For Jhinda Ram had two wives and, naturally, both of them insisted on being called Lady Ram.

Of course, Lalla Jhinda Ram was fairly well able to cope with this crisis in the early stages, as he merely ignored the tension between his wives which began to manifest itself in long sulks and occasional snatches of unmentionable dialogue after the news of the award came through. Jhinda Ram was too busy receiving and answering the numerous congratulations which were arriving, and in his furtive colloquies with that part of himself which did not really believe that he, Jhinda Ram, contractor, whose father was a small shopkeeper, had suddenly been lifted from his five foot five of corpulence to an exalted height equal to that of six foot six Sahib. Apart from the vertical advantages which he had attained, there was the pleasurable feeling of the extension of this personality in girth on the horizontal plane, as it were, through the aura of glory that already radiated from him, as he contemplated himself and smiled to the full-length mirror in stolen side-long glances when none of his servants were looking. As his wives had been wrangling for the last seven years, that is to say, ever since the young, twenty-five-year-old Sakuntala came and ousted the fifty-year-old Sukhi, he regarded their renewed bitterness as only another phase of the quarrel which he had dodged by segregating them in two different parts of his house.

But the quarrel took a serious turn as soon as Jhinda realised that, with the news of the award of Knighthood, there was the invitation to attend the Garden Party which was to be held the next day at the residence of His Excellency the Governor, specially for the ceremony of investiture of all those dignitaries who had been granted titles, medals and scrolls of honour.

For, the invitation which came from Government House was for Sir Jhinda and Lady Ram. And as the new Knight only asked his younger wife, Sakuntala, to buy a new sari and get ready for the occasion, the news of this discrimination travelled through the servants to the part of the house where the old wife, Sukhi, was segregated. And there was trouble.

Perhaps, however, trouble is too mild a word for what happened. For it was a veritable war that broke out in the comparatively peaceful house of Sir Jhinda, and trenches were dug, or rather, barricades raised, and if there was no gunpowder used, it was only because women in India have not yet learnt all the tricks of AI Capone as the men have through the talkies.

The bungalow, in which Lalla Jhinda Ram and his two spouses lived, had been specially built before his second marriage, in the now famous Purdah style which has become current in Hindustan. Its front, which looked out into Lawrence Road, was like the front of an ordinary English bungalow, with a verandah decorated by palm trees and hanging plants, leading through a narrow hall into a large living-room. On either side of this commodious *salon,* were a suite of bedrooms and boudoirs, bounded by a walled square, which was itself divided by a high wall running right through the middle of the compound.

Until the beginning of the war over the question as to who was to be called Lady Ram and go with Sir Jhinda to the investiture at Government House, both Sukhi and Sakuntala had more or less followed a convention not to interfere with each other but to keep to their different households, attended by servants who all lived a common life in a row of one-roomed houses outside the bungalow. Lalla Jhinda Ram slept alternate nights in the suites of the two wives and spent the few hours during which he was at home in the day time in the English style *gol kamara* or, living-room. And life went on smoothly enough, except when these unwritten agreements were violated in any way. Even if there were differences over any undue favour that the lord and master was known, through the gossip of the servants, to be showing to one wife over the other, they were settled through the 'Long sulk method' of boycott or through the malicious gossip campaign conducted with the help of partisan servants or relations. And, as both wives enjoyed an equal status under custom, and the rankling bitterness of the old wife was alleviated by the consideration that her husband had only married a second time for the perpetuation of the race since she was barren, life had passed smoothly enough.

But in the crisis which matured before the investiture, a question of principle suddenly arose. For the English, who still allowed the Hindu *Mitakshara* Law to be practised side by side with the Indian Penal Code which they had imposed, and who, therefore, allowed a man to marry three or four wives, had made no ruling whether all or any of these wives could assume the title of Lady in case the husband was suddenly raised to a Knighthood or Viscountcy, or Earldom, Dukedom or anything like that. The question presented itself to Sukhi, the older wife, that if she was not allowed to call herself Lady Jhinda Ram, she, the less-favoured of the two wives, would lose all the prestige that belonged to her as a *mater familias,* and that she would be as good as thrown on the rubbish-heap in full view of that chit of a girl, Sakuntala, who had so far regarded her as a kind of mother-in-law and been fairly respectful to her.

So, early in the morning, after she heard that Sakunatala alone had been asked by the master of the house to go to the Garden party at Government House, Sukhi outflanked the wall that divided the suite of rooms from her young rival's and walked straight through the English — style living-room and opened her attack.

'Eater of her masters, this is the last humiliation which you had to cast on me!' she began. 'But I'll pull every hair on your head and blacken your face!!!'

Sir Jhinda and Lady Sakuntala Ram had hardly yet awakened from their deep slumber. On hearing., this violent language, they scrambled out of bed, lest Sukhi should really mishandle them.

'Go to your rooms,' Sir Jhinda said peremptorily, rubbing his eyes.

'I will stay here if I like,' said the loud Sukhi. 'I am the owner of the whole of this house. You had nothing before I brought a lakh of rupees in my dowry!... What did this bitch bring with her — nothing but a fair complexion and a snub nose.'

'Go, go, gentle woman!" protested Sakuntala meekly. 'Go to your own part of the house and don't eat my life.

Whereupon Sukhi let loose a flood of curses, imprecations and innuendoes and silenced them both.

Unable to bear the continued flow of her abuse Sir Jhinda ultimately had to resort to *force majeure.* Like a knight of old he summoned the true sense of chivalry towards his young love and, taking Sukhi by the hair, tried to drag her away to her part of the house. Strangely enough the old woman did not respect her lord and master any more, for she resisted like a tiger and, upturning the table in the livingroom, barricaded herself there and waxed eloquent about the misdeeds of Sir Jhinda and Lady Ram all day.

Sir Jhinda was sufficiently perturbed by her stand to go and telephone the A.D.C. to His Excellency the Governor to ask for an appointment to see him on an urgent matter.

The A.D.C., who was busy with arrangements for the Garden Party next day, stalled, presuming that Sir Jhinda Ram was only after some deal or contract as usual, and though the commissions the Sahib had received from this knight had always been generous, Captain Forbes had made his pile and did not want to get involved in these shady negotiations any more.

But as the battle between his two wives was still raging at noon, when Sir Jhinda returned home for the midday meal, the knight was very distressed and thought of a typically Indian and very unorthodox manner of approach to the whole question. Always, in time of trouble in the old days any man could go right up to the king, Sir Jhinda knew; so he would go and see the Governor of the province, the king's representative, the shadow of the monarch.

He had, however, reckoned without his hosts. For, as he drew upto the gates of Government House, the sepoy on sentry wanted to see his pass. And no lies that Sir Jhinda could concoct about his being the contractor, who had to superintend the supply of cutlery for the Garden Party, would satisfy the soldier of the king.

'The Garden Party is in the afternoon', the sepoy said. 'Lat Sahib is at tiffin. And there are strict orders that no one should disturb his siesta.'

Sir Jhinda, humiliated before his chauffeur, got into his car and returned homewards. On the way, he exercised all his wits to discover some way to solve the infernal crisis in which he found himself. But howsoever he looked at the problem, he knew a few things were certain: (1) that Sukhi would never let him rest all his life if she was not called Lady Ram and taken to the Garden party; (2) that Sakuntala would never let him come near her if, after having told her to prepare for the Garden party, he now withheld this pleasure from her; (3) that there was no way of contacting the Governor or A.D.C., and that it was no use seeking advice of any of the gentry in the town, because they would be malicious and make a joke of what was a question of life and death for him.

'Forgive, me, Lallaji', said the chauffeur, turning round as Jhinda Ram got out of the car in the drive of his bungalow, 'forgive me for being so officious as to make a humble suggestion...

'What do you know of all this?' said Sir Jhinda Ram, angry but humble, for he knew his servants knew all about his predicament. 'speak, what have you to say?'

'Maharaj, forgive me who is not good enough to clean the dust of your shoes... But why don't you take both the Bibis to the Party?'

'*Acha*, mind your business,' said Sir Jhinda Ram gruffly, and dismissed the driver.

But in his heart of hearts he thought how obvious and simple a solution to the whole problem this was. Why, if he could marry two wives in law, he certainly ought to have a right to call them both Lady Rams. There was no precedent for this, but he would create the precedent. And, anyhow, the governor could not turn one of his wives out if he took them both to the party. The only difficulty was the invitation card, which was only for Sir Jhinda and Lady Ram... But that was easy. He would alter the words to 'The two Lady Rams', as he had altered many more intricate documents in the past.

'*Ohe*', he called to the chauffeur, 'Go and tell both the Bibis to get ready for the Garden Party. And get my bearer to serve my tiffin.'

With that quality of tact which the driver had displayed to Sir Jhinda, he respectfully approached both the wives and told each of them separately that she alone was going to the garden party. Sakuntala had already been confident about her husband's choice, but Sukhi's vanity was tickled by the special emphasis that the chauffeur laid on the Master's ultimate choice of her. This appeased her wrath for the while, so that she began to prepare for the occasion.

The duplicity of the driver afforded Sir Jhinda enough time to eat his midday meal in peace and even to have his siesta, a bath and a change of clothes. And when the two wives appeared, both dressed in the most flashing saris and found they had been tricked, they dared not, out of respect for their prolonged toilet, gouge each other's eyes out. Besides, the clever driver took charge of them and Sir Jhinda, bundled them into the car and sped towards Government House.

The sentries at the gates of the holy of holies presented arms to the honoured guests as the car slid into the drive.

And, apart from the lifted eyebrows of the butler as he sonorously announced 'sir Jhinda and the two Lady Rams' to His Excellency and Her Excellency, who stood receiving the guests at the head of a marquee, nothing untoward happened. As a matter of fact, Her Excellency made it a point to compliment the two Lady Rams on their wonderful saris, and His Excellency was cordiality itself when he presented the Star of the Knight Commander of the Indian Empire to Sir Jhinda Ram.

There were a few young boys and girls who chuckled as they furtively whispered to each other 'Look there! — the two Lady Rams!' But then the youth of today, in Government House and outside, is notorious for its complete disregard of all manners, codes, conventions, rules and regulations. And such disrespect was only to be expected.

Since that day Sir Jhinda and the two Lady Rams are a familiar feature of all ceremonial occasions in our capital. And no Empire Day, cricket match or horse race is complete without them. For they are three staunch pillars of the Raj which has conceded to them privileges unknown in the annals of the Angrezi Sarkar of India.

19

The Liar*

Labhu, the Shikari of my village, was a born liar. Therefore he had won the reputation of being the best story-teller in our parts. And though a sweeper of low caste, he was honoured by all and sundry. He was tolerated even to the extent of being given a seat at the foot of the banyan tree. And my mother did not insist too harshly on the necessity of my taking a bath to purify myself every time I had been seen listening to one of his uncanny tales with the other village boys.

Labhu was a thin, little man, with the glint of a lance and the glide of an arrow. His wiry, weatherbeaten frame must have had immense reserve of energy, to judge by the way he could chase stags up the steep crags of the hills behind our village and run abreast of the bay mare of Subedar Deep Singh to whose household he was attached as a Shikari, except when some English official, a rich white merchant, or a guest of the Subedar, engaged him for a season. It was perhaps this wonderful physical agility of his that had persuaded him to adopt the profession of a Shikari.

---

* From *The Barber's Trade Union and Other Stories.*

Labhu had also a sensitive, dark face of which the lower lip trembled as it pronounced the first accents of a poignant verse or the last words of a gruesome hunting story. And it was the strange spell that his tragic verses and weird stories cast on me that made me his devoted follower through childhood. He taught me the way to track all the wild animals' and he taught me how to concoct a cock-and-bull story to tell my father if I had to make an excuse for not being at home during the reign of the hot sun.

His teaching was, of course, by example, as I was rather a critical pupil.

'Labhu,' I would say, 'I am sure it is impossible to tract any prey when you are half up the side of a hillock.

'Acha', he would say, 'I will show you. Stand still and listen.' I did so and we both heard a pebble drop. Up he darted on the stony ridge in the direction whence the sound had come, jumping from crag to crag, securing a precarious foothold on a small stone here and a sure one on a boulder there, till he was tearing through a flock of sheep, towards a little gully where a ram had taken shelter in a cave, secure in the belief that it would escape its pursuer.

'All right,' I would say. 'You may have been able to track this ram, but I don't believe that yarn of yours about the devil ram you saw when you were hunting with the Subedar.'

'I swear by God Almighty', he said, 'It is true.' The Subedar will tell you that he saw this terrible apparition with me. It was a beast about the size of an elephant. With eyes as big as hen's eggs and a beard as long as that of Maulvi Shan Din, the priest of the mosque, only not henna-dyed and red, but blue-black; it had huge ears as big as elephant's which did not flap, however, but pricked up like the ears of the Subedar's horse; it had a nose like that of the wife of the missionary Sahib, and it had square jaws which showed teeth almost as big as the chunks of marble which lie outside the temple, as it laughed at the Subedar. It appeared unexpectedly near the peak of Devi Parbat. The Subedar and I had ascended about twelve thousand feet up the mountain in search of game, when suddenly, out of the spirit world that always waits about us in the living air, there was the clattering of stones and boulders, the whistling of sharp winds, the gurgling of thunder and a huge crack on the side of the mountain. Then an enormous figure seemed to rise. From a distance it seemed to both of us like a dark patch, and we thought it was on *oorial* and began to stalk towards it. What was our surprise, however, when, as soon as we saw it stand there, facing us with its glistening, white eyes as a hen's egg, it sneezed and ripped the mountain-side with a kick of its forefeet and disappeared. The mountain shook and the Subedar trembled, while I stood bravely where I was and laughed till I wept with joy at my good luck in having seen so marvellous a manifestation of the devil-god of the tribe of rams. I tell you, son, please God I shall show him to you one of these days.'

'Labhu, you don't mean to say so!' I said, half incredulous, though I was fascinated by the chimaera.

'Of course I mean to say so, silly boy's said Labhu. 'This is nothing compared to the other vision that was vouchsafed to me, praise be to God, when I was on the journey to Ladakh, hunting with Jolly John Sahib.' And he began to relate a fantastic story of a colossal snake, which was so improbable that even I did not believe it.

'Oh, you are a fool, Labhu,' I said. 'And you are a liar. Everybody says so. And I don't believe you at all. My, mother says I am silly to believe your tales.

'All right, then, if you don't believe my stories why do you come here to listen to them?' he said, with wounded pride. 'Go, I shall never teach you anything more, and I shall certainly not let you accompany me to the hunts.'

'All right,' I said, chagrined and stubborn. 'I don't want to speak to you either.'

And I ran home bursting with indignation at having forced a quarrel upon Labhu, when really he only told me his stories for my amusement.

Labhu went away for a while on a hunting tour with the Subedar. He didn't come back to the village when this tour finished, because Subedar Deep Singh's eldest son, Kuldeep Singh, who was lieutenant in the army, took him for a trip across the Himalayas to Nepal.

During this time, though I regretted Labhu's absence, I lent my ear readily to the malicious misrepresentation of his character that the Subedar and his employers, and occasionally also my father, indulged in; because, though superior to Labhu by caste, they were not such good shots as he was.

'He can only wait by a forest pool or a safe footpath to shoot at some unfortunate beast, this Labhu!' said the Subedar. 'And often he shoots in the dark with that inefficient powdergun of his. He is no good except for tracking.

'Yes,' said my father, 'he is a vain boaster and a liar. The only beast be dared to shoot at while he was with me was a hare, and even that he hit in the leg.'

I waited eagerly for Labhu's return to confirm from his very mouth these stories of his incompetence, because, though incredulous of this scandal, I had been driven to a frenzy of chagrin by his insulting dismissal of me. I thought I would ask him point-blank whether he was really as bad a hunter as the Subedar and my father made him out to be.

When Labhu came back, however, he limped about and seemed ill. It was very sad to see him broken and dispirited. And I forgot all the scandal I had heard about him in my bafflement at the sudden change that had come into his character, for he was now no longer the garrulous man who sat telling stories to old men and young boys, but a strangely reticent creature who lay in a stupor all day, moaning and murmuring to himself in a prolonged delirium, except that he occasionally hobbled out with a huge staff in his hand in the evenings.

I was afraid to go near him, because he always wore a forbidding, angry look. But the villagers didn't seem to think there was anything the matter with Labhu, as I heard them say, 'Now that we have no patience with him and his stories, he spends most of his time telling them to himself, the fool!'

I owed a loyalty to Labhu, for I had discovered a kinship in my make-up for all those extravagances for which the Shikari was so well known.

So I went up to him one day, as he lay on a broken string-bed near his mud hut, under the precarious shelter which a young pipal gave him.

'You have returned then, Master Labhu,' I said.

'Yes,' he said, 'I have been back some time, son. I looked for you, but you did not seem to be about. But you know, the man who is slain cannot walk even to his own house. This leg of mine pains me and I can't get about as I used to.'

'What happened to your leg, then?' I asked, realizing that he had forgotten all about our past quarrels and was as kind and communicative to me as before. Did you fall down a cliff or something?'

'No,' he said in a tired voice. And he kept quite for a long while.

'What happened then?' I persisted.

'You know, son,' Labhu began, at first pale and hesitant, then smiling and lifting his eyebrows in the familiar manner of the old days, 'I went away on a hunting tour in the pay of the Subedar's eldest son, Kuldeep Singh, and some of his friends. Well, we went to Nepal through the Kulu valley. They had no experience of hunting in this or in any other part of the world, and I led them across such trails as I knew and such as the local shikaris told me about. That boy, Kuldeep, I don't know what he does in the army, but he can't shoot at any range, and the Sahibs with him were clumsy, purblind white men. I would point to a beast with my stock, and, though they could sèe the hide before their eyes, they bungled with their guns or were too noisy on their feet, and away crashed the bull which we had been tracking. I would grunt, shrug my shoulders and did not mind, because they were like children. They had finished hundreds of cartridges and had not shot anything, and daily begged me to help them to secure some game.

'At first I told them that game doesn't taste sweet unless it is shot by oneself. But at length I took pity on them and thought that I would secure them a good mixed bag. I shot twelve tigers with my gun and fifteen panthers in the course of seven days, and many stags.

'On the eight day we saw a monster which had the body of a wild bear, the head of a reindeer, the feet of a goat, the tail of a wild bull and a glistening, fibrous tissue all round it like the white silken veil which the Rani of Boondi wore when she came to visit Subedar Deep Singh's wife. Kuldeep Singh and the Sahibs were very frightened of this apparition and said it was the devil himself who had the shape of an earthly being and who would soon breathe a breath which would mix with the still air of the night and poison life.

'They were all for killing it outright, while I was sure that I was only a princess of the royal house of Nepal who had been transformed by some magician into this fantastic shape and size. And I wanted to catch it alive and bring it home to be my bride.'

'Labhu went on to relate how beautiful she was and how he resolved to restore her to her normal self by reading magical incantations.

'I told her I loved her,' he continued, 'And she smiled shyly. But some fool, I think it was the Subedar's son, fired a volley of shots, which frightened her so that she ran, became one with the air and began to ascend the snowy peaks of Kailash Parbat.

'I was bent on rescuing my beloved, and I leapt from one mountain to another, calling after her to stop. But that idiot

Kuldeep and the Sahibs kept on shooting and roused the magician who kept guard over her. And this evil sage threw a huge mountain of snow at me to kill me.

'I just blew a hot breath and the mountain of snow cracked into a million pieces and hung about the sky like glittering stars.

'Then the magician struck the earth with his feet and opened up a grave to bury me alive.' I leapt right across the fissure and found myself on a peak in the land of the lama who never dies.

By now, of course, the magician had hidden the beauty away in some cave. So, I gave up the chase, as there was the doom of death about this beauty, anyhow, and I made one leap across the Himalayas for home...'

'And as you landed this side of the mountains you sprained your foot,' I said.

Labhu lifted his eyebrows funnily in the manner of the old days and, laughing, said: 'Have I told you this story before, then?

Part V

PROBING THE MIND

20

The Tamarind Tree*

Ochre red was the colour of the ripe tamarind fruit, bursting out of the green brown shells on the branches of the shady tree in aunt Kesaro's courtyard. And Roopa stared at the bud almost as she had contemplated her own juicy lips in the broken mirror before she became pregnant. She did not know why the saliva filled her mouth. But she felt an irresistible longing for the taste of the sharp, sweet fruit...

She withdrew from where she had sat scrubbing brass utensils with ashes in the open air kitchen of her mother-in-law, and went towards the alcove where her husband kept the mirror. The stolen glance from under the projection of her headcloth showed her the reflection of her pale lips, dried by sighs and the muffled breaths in which she uttered words in answer to others... Perhaps, she had wanted to put on the rich colour of the tamarind to put on the rich ripe colour of the tamarind fruit on her lips and cover the pallid hue. She knew that it was the turmoil in her belly that was creating the wild swirling waves of desire. And the flavour of the tamarind alone could appease her yearning.

---

* From *Lajwanti and Other Stories*

Demurely, she covered her face against possible stares, though her mother-in-law was out washing clothes on the well. Perhaps, 'they' would come home from the office and tease her. This husband of hers was clever, both with words and the way he could steal back home when father and mother were not there, and hug her or bite her lips.

The warm spring air swept the head apron aside with a strong whiff, like that of the first wave of a dust storm. And, again, she found her eyes uplifted to the ripe fruit of the tamarind tree.

The branches of the tree swayed a little. The young mother-to-be also moved on her haunches towards the earthen pitcher, as though the rhythm of work was the same as the swaying of the tree, with the uprush of energy in its waving branches.

The craving for the tamarind in her mouth was renewed.

'But you have just eaten the midday meal, mad one!' she told herself. 'You are not hungry — it is true mother-in-law gives you just enough and no more, but you are not hungry...'

She felt that she was a child again, the way she was longing for the tamarind and talking to herself. Only she could not now venture out into the courtyard of aunt Kesaro, as she had broken all bounds as a girl, jumped, capered, run and climbed trees. Oh for the innocence of girlhood and its abandon! Oh for those afternoons filled with games! And, hai, those companions with whom one quarrelled, only to make up by linking finger to finger...

Oh if only she could now go and get the tamarind cloves which had already fallen on the ground.

As her eyes traced the curve of her longing, she saw aunt Kesaro sitting up from the cot where she had lain under the shade of the tamarind tree. The range of the old woman's vision had been dimmed long ago. And she seemed to blink at the glare of the sun of the afternoon. But her wrinkled face was dry brown black with the anxiety to preserve the fruit of the precious tree against all poachers.

One day Roopa had ventured to pick up a clove of tamarind form the courtyard of Kesaro and the old woman had just let go a torrent of abuse. The sweat had bathed her body, even as he had run home to avoid being caught, and for fear her mother-in-law may have seen her poaching, because Kesaro and her husbands's mother were of like mind about the way the young were going down the drain.

The young woman raised her eyes and contemplated the gnarled face of the hag. The old woman now seemed to be counting coins from her little string purse. No, that could not be, for Kesaro depended on her son and had no money. Perhaps, she was scratching her waist, because of the lice in the pleats of her skirt.

For a moment, Roopa had a terrible premonition which bedewed her nose with jewels of perspiration. She too would some day become old and wretched like this hag, with an obsession that all the young were stealing the fruit from her tree.

And would her strong young husband, with the clipped moustache, become like her father-in-law, a crochety old man, uttering foul words to make his wife generous to her, Roopa?

Just then there was a swirling movement in her belly.

Perhaps the little one was kicking to get out... Let us hope it will be a girl, because then she could dress her in satin, with its lovely sheen. But never mind if it is a boy, because he would bring home a beautiful moon-faced bride...

'Give me a glass of water!" the gruff voice of her husband came.

Did her thoughts bring him home so suddenly? Why?...

How?... But Oh why? ...why?

She pulled the edge of her head apron quickly over her eyes.

'Come, hurry, not so many blandishments!' 'they' were saying.

The sweat covered her face. And her heart drummed for fear. For a moment, she was shivering with the shock.

And then there were swirling movements in her tummy. And, somehow, the thought came to her of the moments of the night when he wanted her blandishments. She had become pregnant, when, on that hot night of end summer, half out of fear and half out of coquetishness, she had evaded him on the top terrace of the house and he had chased her, caught her in his arms and crumpled her on the bed. Oh that night! All the shame had disappeared from her face and she had looked at his strong face, with the hard jaw, relieved by the big black eyes. All the impulses of her youth had flared up into the fire which consumed her and filled her with the insouciance of dreams, before she knew she had gone off to sleep... Oh that night!

She quivered with trepidation in case 'they' should ask her to come inside. And yet she felt the pang of remorse that she had resisted him always. Why, even now she felt the gnawing desire to be with him...

'I would like some tamarind from aunt Kesaro's tree', she breathed the only words which she could mention to evade the longing to be touched by him.

'And I heard you singing with the girls the other day: 'Where have you gone, oh gone away?' he said to her, restraining his voice almost into a whisper.

'I cannot reach the branches', she said ignoring his meaning. 'And, anyhow, the old woman is vigilantly guarding her tree'.

'Come, come inside', he coaxed her.

Only, at that moment, her father-in-law coughed a wheezy cough, ground the phlegm in his throat, and spat out the weight of age in the direction of the tree. And he called:

'The wife of my son — what about my hookah?'

Roopa sighed.

Her husband wheeled on his feet, stamped the earth with the harsh resentment of defeat, twisted his mouth into unuttered speech and went towards his bicycle.

She sat open mouthed, holding the tumbler of water she was going to offer him. And in her upraised right hand there was also a resentment, a spite against the whole world that her inner impulses always remained where they were, incommunicable even to her man.

She felt she wanted to cry. And she covered her face so as not to be seen in her weakness.

She strangled the cry in her belly.

Then she got up and began to prepare the hubble bubble for her father-in-law.

As she blew at the smouldering coal covered by the ashes in the oven, the smoke drew tears from her eyes. And she was gratified that she could pass off her sorrow under cover of the smoke. And her pallid face glowed with the agitation of effort to go towards her father-in-law.

Quickly, she recovered her equanimity after she had placed the hookah before the old man and came back.

At that moment, however, she heard Kesaro shouting:

'That is you? Daughter-in-law of Rakha?.. And what ails you, young woman — that you cannot even produce the child you have been carrying in your belly all these months?... And, in spite of all the tamarind you have stolen and eaten from my tree...'

Roopa wished she could run away — far far away from these cruel harsh words.

But these sentiments were reinforced by the voice of her mother-in-law, who had just then returned from the well.

'Sister, these girls look at the mirror all day! Or they sit about longing for the husband to come back! They don't want to bear the children...'

The young woman reeled as she stood by the kitchen. She felt she might faint. So she rushed towards the inner sanctum of the barn and lay down on the bridal bed that had come in her dowry.

The body with which she had borne the aggravated state of her pregnancy flowered into shooting stars of pain. Almost as though her belly was being churned up... And she tried to think of the softer things which she felt for the forthcoming offspring.

'Moon-faced one-will it be? Or rough? Certainly, it was the creature of violent loving? But she had not eaten enough of the good things which made a child's bones strong? The scanty money of her husband's pay as a peon hardly provided bare bread and lentils... The terrible thought occurred to her: Will the lack of enough nourishment turn the boy into a robber? It may know somehow that it never had enough as a child; and it may wish to revenge itself on others. But, perhaps, if it was a robber it may be like Jagga, the bandit, who robbed the rich to feed the poor and sang in the loveliest words.

Roopa lay prostrate on her bed. The pains now gripped her.

And she tore the ceiling with her shrieks.

The mother-in-law came to her and held her hand, smoothened her straying hair and wiped the sweat form her face. And then she went and called Kesaro who had been midwife at the birth of Roopa's husband.

The shrill cries of the little boy soon tore the quite of the courtyard.

Groups of neighboring women from beyond the tamarind tree came over to greet the newly born.

'May he live long!' old Kesaro said. 'He will give me a tunic of velvet and a silk headcloth.'

'May he not have to beg for food', the mother-in-law of Roopa said to avert the evil eye.

'May he survive.!' a neighbour said grudgingly. 'And may my own daughter-in-law become green!...'

Spring turned into early summer. And that year the tamarind tree bore more fruit then ever. Only Roopa never tasted a clove of this fruit which she had desired — the neighbouring children having looted everything in spite of old aunt Kesaro's vigilance.

But the lips of the young bride were ripe and blood red as she put her mouth to her babe — even though her face was sallow like the leaves of the tamarind tree...

21

The Silver Bangles*

The lines on the corners of her mouth became deeper, the faded texture of her pale face turned livid, and her sleek brows knitted into a frown, as soon as Shrimati Gopi Goel saw the silver bangle on the wrist of the sweeper girl, Sajani...

She drifted away from the kitchen where she was frying sweet bread to please her husband on the first day of the welcome month of rains, shravan, and she took position by the *jallied* window of the living room, overlooking the verandah. She wanted to see what effect Sajani's silver bangle, would have on the owner of the house.

She had seen, passing on his face, the ghost of a smile every time he had seen Sajani arrive. Sometimes, there had been a light in his eyes which she could not help mistaking for a mischievious twinkle. And, once or twice, she felt, she had caught him 'red-handed' or rather 'red-headed', because he had looked up to the untouchable girl with the segment of his lascivious lips slavering and wet, even as he had hummed the phrase of the folk song:

---

* From *Lajwanti and Other Stories.*

"Sajani, I wake up in a hot sweat in the night..."

As she had surmised, she saw from the window the confirmation of his interest in Sajani quite clearly. A smile brimmed over his face, the eyes lit up, the mouth puckered, and he said with a hearty bluff designed to hide exaltation on seeing the girl:

'Ao ji, Ao, come, Sajani, you are late this morning...'

Shrimati Gopi Goel felt her heart throb, in spite of herself, at the intimate strain in her husband's voice as he greeted the sweeper girl, specially in the lilting manner in which he pronounced her name: 'sajaniai...'

She heard the girl respond, shyly draping her headcloth across one side of her face, but with obvious pleasure at being taken notice of, on the other side of her face: 'the rains...

Shrimati Gopi Goel tried to explore the young woman's visage. In the half concealed, half revealed profile, she thought she could detect a radiance, which seemed to rise from the flush of youth, as well as from the vanity of being admired, and the meaningful exaggeration, the emphasis of near song in his pronounciation of her name.

'Oh, Mundu, ask, 'them' to give Sajani a sweet *poora...*' Shri Ram Goel called to the servant boy as he lifted his gaze from the *Tribune* to caress the trim, small crouching figure of the sweeper, girl wielding the broom on the verandah. 'them' will give Sajani everything.' commented Shrimati Gopi Goel.

'Bibiji, I am unworthy,' said Sajani apologetically. 'Master is king to the poor'...

Could she restore between herself and him, asked

Shrimati Gopi Goel in her nerves, the actuality of any connection now. At the end of her heart's echo, there was the sinking feeling that there had been no connection at all.

Only he had taken her after their marriage as a kind of ritual, because the orthodox brotherhood put them on the terrace of the family house in Amritsar by themselves. She had been so frightened. The shame of exposing any part of her body, including her face, instilled into her by her mother had suffused her face with blushes, soaked her clothes in sweat, and she had lain back supinely, offering no resistance and no help. And he had turned away and soon begun to snore... Since then the ritual had been repeated for five years, becoming completely mechanical, without the intervention of words-automatic, like the gestures of old puppets... In spite of this routine, however, because of the commencement of some kind of feeling in her body, which would make her limbs warms and opulent, which would send swirling waves of desire, pushing her from side to side in the ocean of hell, which would torment her in the nights floating in the incandescent air, she would respond with a frightened apathy couched in the form of blandishments of ennui...

Thus her underjaw hardened, her lips were parted, almost as though by a tremor, and her eyes jutted out. She wished she could confront them both with the accusation:

'Lovers!' But she knew that her husband would stave off any direct words with the evasive calm of the practised hypocrite in some neat little phrase from the poem.

To be sure, even without her uttering a sigh, he had scanned her spying figure behind the *jailed* window and recited a made-up verse:

'Ah, between me and this bird here, there stands the shadow of despair...'

'What are you talking about?... I came to say: are you going to get ready to go to office or not?'... Breakfast is ready!!! It is no use having the *pooras* cold!!!

The shrillness of her voice compelled Shri Ram Goel to be sweeter still.

'In this opaque heart of mine, there is only poetry but no office — I hate the outline of that prison...'

'Poetry will not give us bread!...'

'Ah there is no way to tame this shrew', he mumbled and he folded the paper, stole a glance at the shapely curves of Sajani's body, yawned to cover the retreat of his eyes from the innocent pleasure of his ascending soul, and got up.

Shrimati Gopi Goel believed that her husband had deposited bits of his poetaster's soul in her every time he had come near her... And she did not want to allow any of this deposit to be left anywhere else, especially in the body of Sajani, to whom he had already addressed his insinuating love words, in that half-joking, half embarassed manner of the heart-squanderer, even as he deposited on the palm of the sweeper girl's hand occasional tips of money.

As she sat down to make *pooras* for him with her own hands, she fancied the feeling her secret heart, had conferred upon her the right to the exclusive possession of his glances, his words, his embraces, and that none could have the privilege of encroaching upon her vested interests.

'You have burnt every second *poora* for the one you have

made — and anyhow they are all cold,' Shrimati Goel said. 'Let me make them...' She said this to Mundu, as she really wanted to admonish someone just now.

And as though this irritation with the servant boy had heightened her devotion to the fictional image of her husband, she burr-burred:

'I am burning'.

Actually, the hot glow of the fire in the earthen chulha had induced heat in her body, which she mistook for the warmth for him.

'My life,' she said, 'do finish dressing up. You are, standing before the mirror like a bridegroom today...'

'I would not mind going through a marriage, again!' he answered lightly.

'With whom?' She asked, disturbed by the ambiguity of his speech.

'With you', he said, cornered.

This reassured her. She paused for a moment, put all the *pooras* fried so far, back into the pan sizzling with hot butter, and then craning her head to see if he had addressed his remarks to her or to Sajani, she found that the sweeper girl was, in fact in the room where he confronted the looking glass.

She stirred the hot oil with the perforated spoon and, with a histrionic ability far in excess of her usual placid manner she asserted:

'Already, we are one, my life... Already, you have changed me, from my shyness into a wanton... Like Mira, I am the Gopi of my Krishna...'

'I should not seek the Lord in this way, if I were you!' he said cunningly. 'such devotion will bring pain...'

'But, my life-why?' she protested. 'I am your...' She wanted to say. 'I am your servant', but the presence of Mundu prevented her from mouthing his intimate, servile utterance.

'Oh why, Oh why, oh why...' Shri Ram Goel intoned the words, trying to clothe the atmosphere with the aura of a bluff, because he was waiting for the moment when he could meet Sajani's eyes just once before going to the office, so that the day should pass happily, poetically, specially in this lover-like weather, when the clouds hovered over the town, spreading the cool of heaven everywhere and making the green parrots fly in droves towards the freedom of the skies.

'But why?' she insisted. 'Why will my devotion bring more pain?'

'Because, in one of the two, who have become one, takes it into his head to depart, as when you suddenly decide to go to your mother's home in a sulk, the pain which this causes is the most virulent disturbance... There is an emptiness in one's life. And the partner who is left behind has to try to fill the vessel again with nectar...'

This profound decorative speech was made in so deliberately light-hearted a voice that Shrimati Goel was amused flattered and reassured.

At the moment, she saw Shri Ram Goel pressing a ten paisa coin on the palm of Sajani. Actually, he had merely placed the coin on the sweeper girl's open hand and not pressed it. But the insensate imagination of Shrimati Goel fancied as though this act of charity had established the connection of love between those two in a final and clear manner. She even thought that she had seen them exchange glances which were like shooting stars.

The wife felt like upsetting the cauldron of boiling butter on the heads of the two lovers. But the imperturbable calm on the countenance of Shri Ram Goel offset any such wild action. Instead, she dipped her head coyly and cooed to him like an innocent lover.

'I am going to give you the *pooras* fried with my own hands-not those done by Mundu!'... Did you notice the silver bangles on that low woman's wrist! How she preens herself-this sweeper! I wish her mother would come to do our house and not this film star.

The eyelids of Shri Ram Goel dipped before these words. He carried the hot *pooras* to his mouth and pretended to have burnt his tongue. And he rolled his eyes with a mock humour to cover his retreat from the defence of his innocence and poetry to the fool's paradise where the illusion of marriage must go on, so that Shrimati Gopi Goel may believe that she was his only love, his otherself, the better half.

'And what about the silver bangles you are wearing?... Which lover has given them to you?' Shrimati Gopi Goel asked Sajani as though her mouth was that of a loud policeman's.

'Bibiji, we survive by your grace...' Sajani said meekly.

'God is looking down on the oven of fire in your heart, and he will condemn you to burn in the hell of your own making, if you don't look out!', Shrimati Gopi Goel challenged the girl.

'Hai Bibiji — What have I done?' the sweeper girl sighed and turned pale.

'What have you not done? You have seduced all the men of the neighbourhood with your smiles. 'Bag of dirt that you are! And you ask me innocently 'What have I done?'

From the hot air of the kitchen, the blue anger of Shrimati Gopi Goel travelled like sparks of fire and thus hung in the atmosphere like festoons of smoke over the trembling figure of Sajani.

'My mother brought the silver bangles — they are the first offering for my betrothal!' the untouchable girl explained. And then she looked up to the mistress with her nose bedewed with perspiration, her frank forehead clear, and her eyes filled with tears of innocence accused of guilt by someone.

'Lies won't help to make you people honest!' charged Shrimati Gopi Goel. 'Let me see if these were not stolen from my house...'

Sajani put her hand forward.

'How can I be sure that this profligate husband of mine, who is so generous to you, has not taken them out of my box of jewellery and given them to you.'

'Bibiji', protested Sajani.

Shrimati Goel answered without listening:

'I know the kind of lovers who look separate, but are drawn by the invisible words of mock poems, and who indulge in all the extravagances of connection, without an embrace...'

'I only like to hear Babuji talk' the girl said. 'He is a learned man and speaks so many fine words...'

'Don't you be familiar with me and talk of his fine words you like to hear!!! Only take off those silver bangles which he has stolen from my box and given to you!"

The perfume of Shri Ram Goel's words evaporated before the disillusioned gaze of Sajani. She realised that she should never have uttered her admiration for the Master of the house. Their eyes had once met. But she was not guilty. Her head swirled. And she crumpled up in a swoon on the floor.

'Get up and go out and don't you come into this house again. You have raised your head to the sky — low people, wearing silver bangles!!! Don't your know that untouchable in the south are not supposed to wear silver at all... And you go posing like a cheap film star... Go die!'

Sajani had lost the use of her muscles, but not of her heart. She began to sob as she sat huddled in a corner of the verandah. But each movement of her throat was like a knife jab, bringing more sobs, as though the fainting fit had been succeeded by hysteria, the sobs welling from the belly where lay years of humiliations, now thrusting up like daggers on her sides.

The sorrow of the sweeper girl made Shrimati Gopi Goel more angry.

'Go, get out and never enter this house again! Thief! You have not only stolen the bangles, but also my—'

She dared not finish her harsh words, because the

acknowledgement of the loss of her husband to Sajani might turn out to be the confirmation of the fact-and that would be inauspicious, because if you say that', it often comes...'

Sajani lifted her head as a dove updives off the earth to fly across the valley, threatened by a rough wind...

22

The Thief*

The 'hoom' of the summer months in India is inexplicable, except in terms of an arilessness which seems to dissolve everything about one slowly and surely into a vague nothingness. Perhaps only a graph could illustrate it, because it is as much a sound effect as sense data, and sound can be drawn. Or, may be, one could dispose certain daubs of paint in such a way as to break the exact symbolism of the Wheel of Life in a Tibetan scroll, and show all the concrete objects falling away, crumbling like the edges of the earth on judgment day, the stars breaking, the comets shaking, the seas full of fire and the Sun alone standing there on high, a magnificent orb of brightness; A cruel, blood-sucking demon, scorching all sentient things as in some prehistoric war of the elements...

Ganesh always felt the listessness of half death when he got up in the mornings, the heavy lids on his eyes literally ached as they opened, and no amount of stretching would stir the cells of his body into a sense of more than the doubt that he existed. So he generally crawled out of bed and proceeded towards the small balcony on the first floor of his ancestral

---

* From *The Tractor and the Corn Goddess and Other Stories.*

mansion, there to inhale deep breaths of any air that was going. But there was seldom even a movement of a: leaf or a dust speck such as could be called a breeze. Only the 'hoom' mixed here with certain asafoetid smells which rose from the open drains of damp lanes, the smoke of centuries and the rubbish of days that like a sore out of the huge bin on the corner of Gupta Road (named after his family) and King George's Road (named after George V, 'the Sailor King,' who stood enshrined in marble fifty yards away in his coronation robes).

Although the 'hoom' persisted and there was no fresh air to breathe, there was a good reason why Ganesh Prashad reappeared to the balcony with such unfailing regularity. For, since the scarcity in the South, the town's population had swelled with beggars, and among these was a woman with a child who had taken shelter on the marble steps at the foot of old King George's statue.

The slippery pads of her buttocks swayed before his gaze in zig-zags, as she walked away from the rubbish bin to the steps of the statue, after collecting a crust or a raw vegetable peel to chew. And as she drifted about like this, Ganesh felt a yearning in his blood, and his breath came and went quickly, until he was nearly in the utter hush of the mornings with the heat produced by the maddening waves of desire. His aching eyelids ached more sharply in the blinding glare and yet he could not keep his eyes from groping across the blaze, among the group of people who clustered round the steps of the statue or the rubbish bin, for the form with the swaying hips.

The fascination had been overwhelming from the start, for the first impression of the triangle formed by her things had made his sensations swirl in a giddy wave. But the memory of this impact had been sucked in by the sagging nerves of his sleep doped body, and had gradually become a vague reaction with which other elements had mingled.

For instance, he had felt a distinct wave of nausea cum pity when he had seen her pick up a rotten banana peel from the rubbish bin and lick it. And he had wanted to run down and tell her that she would get cholera if she ate anything out of that bin. But he was afraid that if he went and singled her out for sympathy the other beggars might notice him and beat him up, for they still seemed to have enough strength left to guard the honour of their women-folk vigilantly. And as he could not do much about it he had just stood and stared at her, with the dull thud of an ache at the back of his head.

On another day, Ganesh had seen the beggar woman feeding her child on a bared breast. And that had aroused a feeling of unbearable tenderness in him, a tenderness, however, which gnawed at his vitals and aroused a lust of which the nether point was fixed somewhere in the memories of his own childhood.

And later, all these feelings had mixed with yet another — with a disgust he had suddenly felt on imagining her unwashed, dishevelled body in his arms, the putrid sore of her mouth touching his, the mouth which had eaten dirt and the filth of the rubbish bin, which had drunk the scum of the drains.

And yet, in spite of all the contradictory feelings, the first fascination of her swaying buttocks lasted, and the irresistible feeling which spread the confusion of a cloud over his senses, so that time and space ceased to exist and no consideration of duty or shame baulked his drunken gaze. And under the impulse of this distended desire, he would stand fixed to the balcony the whole morning though he be late for the office, until his elder brother, with whom he worked in the family firm of solicitors, began to notice the waywardness of his behaviour.

Once, he had tried to work up enough audacity to attract the woman's attention. But, being a timid, respectable creature, he had to summon all the crazy impulses in his being to exercise the demons of destruction in him and beckon them to help him. The whole thing was a joke, he had sought to tell himself, the whole world was a joke and nothing was really stable. He himself, inheriting half the wealth of his dead father, was yet a slave to all the inhibitions and prohibitions of his elder brother and sister-in-law, living a confined, conventional life contrary to everything he had learnt at college, and in full view of the disintegration, death and disease about him. And if it was all a joke, then this woman was a leer, an abject, worthless nothing, an ignorant, illiterate and dumb creature except that she possessed a pair of hips like boulders, the swaying of which excited him and from which he might get the pleasure of a moment, a mere particle of time in the long aeons of eternity where nothing counted or mattered. But, though the need for hypocrisy and circumlocution to build up an argument resulted in coining of a number of euphemisms, he could not get away from the basic human feelings of pity and tenderness.

For, every day he was reminded of the incident in his youth when he had accused a beggar, who used to come up the lane on the right hand side of this house, of stealing a silk dhoti from his study on the ground floor, and had stood by while the servants beat up the beggar. In his younger days he had willed himself into the belief that he had actually seen the beggar rush out of his room with the dhoti, but since then he had felt less and less sure about it, and was, in fact, convinced that he had been guilty of snobbery with violence against an innocent man. And how, this hangover of an unkind act against one beggar had become an undertone beneath the lust for another, and the mingling of these made for a restlessness which was obvious in the increasingly frequent nervous twitch of his neck.

As he stood there one day, he felt he could not bear it. He could see the woman's breasts undraped, where her sari had slipped off as she crouched by the statue and washed the grit out of her child's eyes. And he felt the rustling of a strange song in his ears, the loam-song of dizzy desire mounting to the crescendo of a titanic choir. And the flow of a passionate warmth spread from his loins upwards to his eyes, making them more heavy-lidded and soporific than they had been when he had just awakened.

For long moments he tried to check his instinct to look deeper, to caress the amplitude of her haunches, an instinct which was driving him crazy. But he could feel her presence inflaming his body like a slow forest fire, which comes creeping up from the roots like smoke but becomes a wild red blaze suddenly in one crucial moment.

And as he was choked with desire, his neck twitched like that of a snake in the burning forest, and his vision was clouded altogether. Breathing heavily, hot, suffocated, he lifted his elbows from the wooden railings on which they rested and tried to steady himself.

The woman had now picked up her child and was feeding him at her right breast as she sat cross legged on the ground. But the little one was whining, and shrieking, partly from the pain he had felt at having the thick crusts of grit removed from his eyes, but mainly because there was hardly any milk in his mother's breasts.

Ganesh's passion seemed to congeal as he heard the cries; he could feel an almost tangible loosening of his flesh, and though he was still soporific he realised that he must go and bathe and dress.

But, even as he was withdrawing his gaze after a furtive stare at her haunches, he saw her hit the child with the palm of her hand and trust the nipple of her left breast into the mouth of her son. As Ganesh lingered to see what her second breast looked like, he heard the child yelling continuously. And, now, as though it were a revelation, the fact dawned upon him that there was no milk in the woman's breasts, and that her child, who gnawed at her like a hungry rat, was shrieking with the need of his young life for sustenance.

He stood tense, as though he had a vision, and his head was bent with a humility such as he had never known before, a craven, abject feeling of shame that a mother should have to hit her child in his presence because she had no milk in her breasts to give him, that she should have no milk because probably she had no food herself. The joke, if it was a joke, the leer of her mouth, as well as the general ridiculousness of the world, was far too grim a joke to be merely laughed at. And, though she was unknown to him, an utter stranger, here today and dead tomorrow, she concerned him, if only because he had allied himself in his mind with desire for her.

As soon as the passion had become compassion in his body he had decided upon a course of action.

He turned round with a face knotted as though with revulsion against himself, and rushed downstairs towards the kitchen. It was just possible that by some miracle his sister-in-law might still be having her bath or lingering over her prayers. If so, he could get to the storeroom and get out a bag of grain and give it to the woman and her family on the steps of the statue.

When he got to the kitchen, he found that the course was, indeed, clear. There was only Biju, the servant boy, peeling vegetables there. But the storeroom was locked and the keys, ostensibly, hung at one end of his sister-in-law's sari.

'Where is Bibiji?' he asked the servant impetuously. 'she is having a bath,' Biju said, Ganesh swayed histrionically as though to yawn and stretch in order to bluff the boy. Then he drifted away up the stairs towards the bedroom occupied by his brother and sister-in-law. His brother would be away on his morning's constitutional in the garden, and, with luck, his sister-in-law had undressed in the bedroom and left her bunch of keys there.

With beating heart and anxious face he sneaked into his brother's bedroom and looked around. He was lucky. The bunch of keys was on the dressing table. He took it.

But, before rushing down with it, as the wild cries of the begger woman's child were terrorising him to do, he sought to cover his manoeuvre and to give himself time. He went towards his room and called out:

'Will you be long in the bathroom, sister-in-law?' He knew that she would be longer out of sheer cussedness if only he showed any anxiety to make use of the bathroom.

'Yes, I am washing my hair,' came the answer.

Ganesh's face coloured with glee at the success of his ruse. The only thing that remained was to get the servant boy out of the way. So he called out from the inner balcony:

Biju, go and get me a packet of razor blades from the shop... 'Here's a rupee coming down.'

The servant boy knew that he could always keep any change that was left over from a rupee when Ganesh Sahib sent him shopping. He came eagerly enough into the compound and, picking up the money ran.

Ganesh went down quickly and opened the lock of the storeroom door. He felt he heard a chorus of accusing voices and paused for a moment, but realised that it was only his heart pounding against his chest. And though he could not remember the shrill cries of the beggar woman's child any more, he remembered the way the little rat nibbled at his mother's breasts. For a moment he felt a fool going into the storeroom, a place where he had seldom entered. But then he plunged into the dark.

His brother had hoarded quite a few bags of wheat and rice. So it was not difficult to spot them. Only, he didn't know whether it would be a bag of wheat or rice that he would be taking away. He did not pause to deliberate any more, however. He merely strained to get a grip on the nearest bag.

After rubbing his hands, which were moist with

perspiration, on his pyjamas, he caught hold of the bag and lifted it coolie-wise on his back. Then he scrambled out and made for a small alley on the side of the house.

Hardly had he got to the middle of the passage way when he met Biju, who had come back after buying the razor blades.

'Let me carry it, Babuji, let me carry it,' the boy said. Ganesh was in a panic.

'Get away, get away,' he said.

But as the boy persisted, he thought that he might as well give the load to Biju, as, at any rate, he himself wouldn't look too dignified crossing the stretch between the opening of the gulley and the crowd of beggars by the statue.

'Where shall I take it?' Biju said.

'Give it to the beggars out there,' Ganesh said.

The servant boy looked askance but obeyed the orders. Ganesh returned towards the storeroom to lock it up and restore the keys to his sister-in-law's dressing table.

'Where are my keys?' he heard a voice. But he thought that it was his own bad conscience shouting as it had done before.

'Who has taken the keys? Biju? Where are you? Have you taken my keys?'

Ganesh could not now mistake the source of the voice.

He drifted away from the storeroom door and ambling along as though he had come from a leisurely session in the lavatory below, he said:

'The storeroom is open. Your keys are lying here. Of course, the servant must have taken them...'

His heart beat like a tom in hell now that he had lied.

And he cursed himself for his lack of self-control.

The sister-in-law returned to her room, thinking that the servant had, indeed, taken the keys to get some condiments out of the storeroom.

Ganesh waited for Biju to come back, so that he could conspire with the servant boy to cover up what he had done.

'Don't tell Bibiji about the bag of grain' he said when the boy returned. 'And where are the blades?'

Biju showed him both the blades and the change on the palm of his hands.

'Keep the change,' Ganesh said. And he proceeded upstairs.

Like all people who try to be cleaver and hatch plots to carry out a design, he forgot to do one or two things which were essential to bluff his sister-in-law. For instance, he did lot tell the servant boy the details of his plan about the bag of grain. Nor did he ask him to pretend that he, Biju, had taken the keys from the mistress's table to open the storeroom door and get some condiments out. And when his sister-in-law arrived downstairs and asked for the keys, the servant boy innocently said he knew nothing about hem.

Of course, on sensing the real nature of the situation, he began to invent a lie to the effect that he had taken the keys from Ganeshji to fetch an empty bag out.

The lady of the house, was nothing if not a shrewd, knowing housewife, instinctively aware of the subterfuges, lies and innuendos of all the members of the household. She caught the servant boy in the trap of prevarications that he had begun to make. And, when, on top of incriminating evidence which Biju gave against himself Ganesh said he had seen him carry a bag of grain out of the house, the lady got her husband to beat the servant boy and throw him out, so that he could be free to join the beggars outside, whom he loved so dearly. In spite of the many more lies he told, the servant boy was, however, throughout, as stubborn in refusing to tell upon Ganesh as this gentleman was in concealing the truth which might have cleared up the matter.

The imperturbable calm of Ganesh's behaviour after this incident was only broken when he saw the beggar woman again the next morning. His neck twitched more furiously, and his heavy-lidded eyes blinked, as if someone were digging pins into them, especially because he saw the servant boy, Biju, seated by her almost as though he had taken complete charge of her.

More Indian Fairy Tales (Bombay, 1961).

CRITICAL STUDIES OF THE SHORT STORIES OF MULK RAJ ANAND

Chapters in Books

Gupta, G.S.B., Mulk Raj Anand, *A Study of his fiction in Humanist Perspective* (Bareilly, 1974).

Naik, M.K., *Mulk Raj Anand* (New Delhi, 1973).

Sinha, K.N., *Mulk Raj Anand* (New York, 1974).

Venugopal, C.V. *The Indian Short Story in English: A Survey* (Bareilly, 1975).

Articles

Fisher, M., "*The shape of Lostness*: Mulk Raj Anand's Short Stories', Journal of Indian Writing in English, II, i. 1974.

Gupta, G.S.B., "*Woman in Anand's Shorter Fiction*" Karnataka University Journal, Humanities, XIII, 1969.

Naik, M.K., "*The Plough and the Tractor*: The Short Stories of Mulk Raj Anand", Karnataka University Journal, Humanities, XVI, 1972.

Venugopal, C.V:, "*The Short Stories of* Mulk Raj Anand", Karnataka University Journal, Humanities, XV, 1971.

Lightning Source UK Ltd.
Milton Keynes UK
UKOW01f1557130917
309109UK00006B/277/P

Selected Bibliography

SHORT STORIES BY MULK RAJ ANAND

The Lost Child and Other Stories (London, 1934).

The Barber s Trade Union and Other Stories (Bombay, 1944).

The Tractor and the Corn Goddess and Other Stories (Bombay, 1947).

Reflections on the Golden Bed and Other Stories (Bombay, 1953).

The Power of Darkness and Other Stories (Bombay, 1959).

Lajwanti and Other Stories (Bombay, 1966).

Between Tears and Laughter (New Delhi, 1973). *Selected Stories* (Moscow, 1955).

STORIES RETOLD

Indian Fairy Tales (Bombay, 1946). *Aesop's Fables* (Bombay, 1960).